Darcy watc ... rt and Courtn ... ther as if drawn by powerful magnets. It hit her right between the eyes. Curt and her radiant little sister?

Well, it didn't have *her* blessing. He bent his shapely head and kissed Courtney's apple-blossom cheek. He hugged her. He *did* hug her.

Courtney went very sweetly into Curt's arms, not even reaching his heart. Darcy's own heart gave a great sick lurch. Some trembling voice inside her began to shriek. *Don't take him. He's mine. He's mine. He's always been mine.*

Darcy felt herself flush a hot red. It was all her own fault. She had blundered through her love life. Maybe Courtney was in search of a husband? No woman in her right mind would overlook Curt. But Curt was *her* rock and she couldn't bear to see another woman in his arms. Even her own sister. Her own sister worst of all!

Margaret Way takes great pleasure in her work and works hard at her pleasure. She enjoys tearing off to the beach with her family at weekends, loves hunting galleries and auctions and is completely given over to French champagne "for every possible joyous occasion." She was born and educated in the river city of Brisbane, Australia, and now lives within sight and sound of beautiful Moreton Bay.

Look for the continuation of ***The McIvor Sisters***
in ***Marriage at Murraree***
Coming October 2005
Harlequin Romance® #3863

Books by Margaret Way

HARLEQUIN ROMANCE®

3767—RUNAWAY WIFE*
3771—OUTBACK BRIDEGROOM*
3775—OUTBACK SURRENDER*
3803—INNOCENT MISTRESS
3811—HIS HEIRESS WIFE
3823—THE AUSTRALIAN TYCOON'S PROPOSAL

HARLEQUIN SUPERROMANCE®

762—THE AUSTRALIAN HEIRESS
966—THE CATTLE BARON
1039—SECRETS OF THE OUTBACK
1111—SARAH'S BABY*
1183—HOME TO EDEN*

*Koomera Crossing miniseries

MARGARET WAY

The Outback Engagement

The
McIvor Sisters

TORONTO • NEW YORK • LONDON
AMSTERDAM • PARIS • SYDNEY • HAMBURG
STOCKHOLM • ATHENS • TOKYO • MILAN • MADRID
PRAGUE • WARSAW • BUDAPEST • AUCKLAND

ISBN 0-373-03859-3

THE OUTBACK ENGAGEMENT

First North American Publication 2005.

This edition published by arrangement with Harlequin Books S.A.

www.eHarlequin.com

Printed in U.S.A.

CHAPTER ONE

DARCY walked quietly across the Persian rug towards the still figure in the massive canopied bed. The bed was a monstrosity really, elaborately carved and wide enough to sleep a half a dozen but her father was very attached to it. It had once been the property of a McIvor Scottish ancestor. Her father's eyes were closed, his face the dreadful grey that spoke of severe physical trauma. A fuzz of mottled grey and marmalade coloured hair showed at the neck of his pyjamas lending a peculiar vulnerability. The once powerful hands that could handle anything from the wildest brumby and the biggest bullock to every kind of station machinery rested like fleshless talons on the folded top sheet.

Splendid health had accompanied Jock McIvor all the days of his life now he was a wraith of his former self. Almost overnight, the flesh had dropped off his impressive frame. His nurse, Wilma Ainsworth, an angular white-clad figure, competent but not particularly motherly or compassionate had been and gone taking with her the tray that held the medicines and syringes to bring temporary relief to her suffering patient.

Big Jock McIvor had not recovered from his first heart attack as everyone had expected. Jock McIvor was dying. Of that there could be no doubt. As she leaned over his prone figure Darcy hardly dared draw breath for fear of waking him out of his drug induced slumber. She withdrew to the wide verandah that enclosed the homestead on three sides. Like everyone experiencing a crisis she desperately wanted to change things. To turn back the clock. To insist on her father having regular medical checkups, knowing he had never been ready to listen to her anyway. Jock McIvor was a law unto himself. It was a strategy that in the end hadn't worked in his favour.

Darcy stared out over the extensive homestead grounds with their magnificent date palms and diverse array of desert plants. The palms had been planted well over a century before by a Afghan camel driver her great great grandfather Campbell McIvor had befriended. Midafternoon the grounds were shrouded in the quivering white fire of a heat haze. It caused a legion of parrots in their glorious colours to descend on the lagoon at the foot of the homestead for a drink. Otherwise the home compound bore a strangely deserted air. Jock McIvor was no longer in charge and it was manifestly obvious. She had been neglecting her duties while she attended her father after that first frightening heart attack. In these last stages despite his agitated protests she'd been forced to call in a full time nurse.

Curt had flown over from Sunrise to urge her to do it. Curt Berenger was another one who was a law unto himself especially since the death of his own father in a helicopter mustering accident leaving Curt master of Sunrise Downs and the entire Berenger chain. Though she found numerous ways of telling him how interfering he was, the truth was Curt followed his family's tradition of looking after his friends and neighbours in time of need. Not that he was an admirer of Jock McIvor. Their relationship was as strained as it could be with her in the middle. Curt saw her father as a tyrant who'd had far too much influence shaping her life. Part of her recognised that. Her father was very controlling but the things Curt said cut her to the quick. Things do when there's a basis in truth.

Now Jock McIvor was dying and she was about to be abandoned again. What a long terrible struggle she'd had with that first abandonment. A double whammy. Mother and sister. She could never put the wrenching psychic separation, the painful moods of loneliness and not being loved behind her. She still saw their tearful faces in her dreams. She had loved Courtney with all her heart assuming they were going to be the closest, dearest friends forever. Her mother had always promised her a baby sister. Everything should have been perfect but in the end the dream had been shattered. Childhood innocence had been replaced by painful moods of sadness and loneliness. How had she lived through her adolescence with no mother present? By becoming what her father wanted. She had lived off the dollops of affection he handed out like the desert flora survives on rare showers.

Anxiety was having the effect of a steel band tightening around her head. Fit as she was, many long sleepless nights had exhausted her. Nurse Ainsworth always urged her to go to bed saying she would wake her if she saw the need, but Darcy was not happy with that. This was her *father.* He was all she had. Didn't the woman realize that? She *had* to be there at her father's side. She sensed she would know the *exact* moment when all life would leave him.

What then?

What will my life become? She sought to push back all thoughts of *freedom* as a betrayal but it continued to hover on the periphery of her mind. She had never known real freedom. By fair means or foul—she became agitated when she thought about it—her father had tenaciously kept her tied to his side. After his marriage break up he had made it a purpose in life. She could understand it in a way. He was a proud man who had suffered bitter losses. Worse, he had been publicly humiliated. Now he was waiting to die and the atmosphere was charged with powerful emotions.

She couldn't run Murraree by herself. It was a big job, not an Outback adventure. Her father had been King of the Castle. The Boss. Jock McIvor always made the decisions. As efficient as he had trained her to be, essentially she carried out orders. What would happen to Murraree with her father gone? She knew the men liked and respected her. Some of them had watched her grow up. She knew how to handle herself, but she wasn't a hard, tough man in a hard, tough man's country.

"You can't cure yourself of being a woman, Darcy," Curt had told her, a kind of pity in his eyes. "Don't you realize you define yourself in relation to your father? It's high time you started being your own person, your own *woman.*"

Curt refused to allow her to avoid issues. Just one of the reasons their arguments were legion. Fighting was a protection against feeling. A way of protecting herself against the pain of a dream that had never come true. Sometimes she didn't know if she loved Curt or hated him. He made her so angry, upset, mad, excited. Wide swings of mood from turmoil to elation. It was like being on a swing, soaring skywards then falling back to earth. Too often she submerged her tempestuous feelings in defying him. It made it that much easier for her to keep control. That was her lot in life. Keeping control.

Now she had to watch her father make his exit from life. It was an eerie experience, rather like a nightmare from which she would surely wake up. Jock McIvor's heart attack at fifty six had not only rocked her to her core, it had rocked the entire Outback. Jock McIvor was in his way a legend. Millionaire cattle man, lady killer, sportsman (only a year before he had still been enjoying his favourite game of polo), raconteur, owner of an historic cattle station with its rambling old homestead that had in its heyday, to be strictly honest, her grandfather's day, hosted many a visiting dignitary and V.I.P. Her father was a true bush identity though Darcy was painfully aware some people described him as a *ruthless bastard.* Still Jock McIvor was known the length and breadth of Outback Queensland and into the Northern Territory.

Unbelievably only six months before he had been a marvellous looking man, still outrageously handsome with flashing blue eyes, wonderful white teeth and a leonine mane that had slowly turned tawny from its once copper glory. Darcy had many fond memories of sitting around the camp fire listening to her father recount his stories to a fascinated audience who hung on his every word. On the down side it had to be said her father had been a hard-drinking, hard-living womaniser. There was no getting away from it. He was a big man with big appetites. It had been a problem. It once caused a crisis when photos surfaced of Jock and a well-known station wife caught in a public display of *affection* for want of a better word. The wronged husband had threatened a shotgun solution. Jock who had a lawless streak in him had only laughed when his daughter had been saddened and deeply embarrassed.

Yes, Jock McIvor had generally been acknowledged to be larger than life. Darcy had thought him invincible.

"When no man is!" Curt again. The entire Outback community knew Darcy and Curt had a powerful attachment both sought to play down. People argued there didn't seem to be any rational explanation for why they were not together. Except maybe Jock McIvor's running interference. They all knew Jock wasn't a man to *share.*

A small sound from the bedroom tore Darcy from her troubled reverie. Her father was stirring, a whistling moan on his breath.

"Dad!" For once she didn't bother with the "Jock" her father preferred her to call him. In the stress of the moment she didn't care. She *was* a woman. Damn it! Emotional.

By the time she reached the bed her father's eyes were

opening slowly, painfully, as though it cost him a great effort. "Darcy." His brow puckered. "Here as usual?"

Something about the way he said it took her aback. "Where else would I be?" She touched his hand tenderly willing herself not to cry. Her father hated tears so much sometimes she thought she had almost lost the ability to cry. She had been brought up to be brave, ignoring her sensitive female side as she tried to turn herself into the heir her father had always wanted yet somehow for all his dalliances had failed to produce.

"I'm finished, girl." It was said flatly, without acceptance. More a hard digust that in former days would have been rage.

She was helpless to deny it. "Dad, I love you so much."

"That's the way you are. Loyal." He fixed his sunken eyes on a life size portrait across the room. It had been painted not long before the inexorable break-up of the family. Two young girls about twelve and ten in immaculate riding gear, white silk shirts and fitted jodhpurs leaned towards a ravishingly pretty, blonde woman who was seated on a burgundy leather couch, similarly attired.

Dress for the portrait had been decided upon by Jock. Marian McIvor hadn't cared for horses or riding. Courtney had followed suit. Courtney, an adorable miniature version of her mother had her arm around her mother's waist. Darcy was perched like some long legged brolga on the arm of the couch, long straight dark hair falling over one shoulder, slanting aquamarine eyes staring gravely out at the viewer.

It had always seemed to her her colouring looked startlingly out of place beside Jock's benchmark of beauty, the enchanting gold and blue of her mother and sister. From family photographs she knew she resembled her long dead paternal grandmother who had been famous for her stoic resilience and everyday heroisms in a vast lonely harsh environment. She even bore her grandmother's maiden name, D'Arcy.

"You were always the serious one." Her father gave a muffled groan, the marks of suffering all over him. "Look at you there. Poker faced. Beside your mother and sister you look damned nearly plain. But you were always as smart as a tack and you've been good. So good. I haven't appreciated you enough. You were the one I could always trust."

Sometimes the things her father said Darcy found horribly wounding. Anything but vain, she knew she was far from plain but her father had never wanted to accept her attractiveness or femininity. Perhaps as Curt continually pointed out her father saw great danger in allowing her to realise her womanly potential.

Father and daughter continued to stare at the portrait, one feeling a sense of attachment, the other, God knows what!

"Why have you always kept the portrait in your room?" Darcy felt driven to ask. Her father's harsh views were entrenched in her consciousness. Jock had always claimed he despised Darcy's mother for leaving him, yet he opened his eyes on her first thing in the morning and closed his eyes on her at night.

"It's the way it's got to be!" A grim smile lifted the corner of Jock McIvor's mouth. "I keep it, Darcy, to remind me what Marian did to me. She sucked all the love from my system. She should never have left me. It was cruel and it was wrong."

"You didn't try hard enough to get her back, Dad. You let them go." The words were torn from Darcy like a bandage from a wound.

"It was your mother's *duty* to return to me." The gaunt face worked, the talons on the white sheet tensed. "When she refused I was *finished* with her. No woman makes a fool of Jock McIvor. A wife should follow her husband everywhere. She knew what she was getting into when she married me, what she had to accept. She was a *bad* wife." His expression was at once bitter and bereft.

"Why didn't she want to take me?" Darcy's plaintive eyes

were fixed upon her mother's painted face. How many million times had she asked herself the question?

Her father shot her a peculiar glance. One she missed. "She wanted Courtney, the pretty one made in her own image. That was the deal. You were the changeling with your dark hair and those slanty eyes. Your mother and your sister subjected us to a massive betrayal, girl. Then she had the hide to punish me with an outrageous divorce settlement when *she* was the one to move out. Remarried, the faithless bitch. You know she wanted you to go to the wedding?"

For a minute Darcy looked at him blankly. "Oh...Dad, you've never mentioned this before." The admission devastated her. She was left with the sick hollow feeling there might be many things her father had never told her when she had given him all her loyalty and trust.

"For God's sake, be your age!" he said, anger seething behind his eyes. "There are lots of things I never told you. Because you didn't need to know. The two of us had to cast your mother and sister aside to survive. Your mother was the enemy. We had to resist her with all our strength. Fact is, Courtney still remains *my* child. Your mother destroyed our relationship but now I'm dying I've had to confront certain issues. Because you've been the one to stay with me doesn't mean I'm going to leave you Murraree, girl. It would take more than a woman to run it."

Darcy took a deep breath, feeling like she had been plunged headfirst into a powerful disbelief. "What are you saying? Murraree is my home. My heritage. I know you've always wanted a son but haven't I demonstrated my love for the land? I've worked long and hard. I carry my weight. If I can't handle the station all on my own, there's always a good overseer." The idea of losing her birthright was absolutely intolerable.

"Overseer!" Jock McIvor rallied to spit out the word. "Damn it all, girl. When I'm gone men will try to take advantage of you. Don't you realise that? How are you supposed to protect yourself? They'll be after you like vultures, not for *you,* but the station."

Darcy studied her father with the shutters all but fallen from her eyes. "I'm confident I can manage my own life, Dad. Murraree might be a top station but I haven't been short of marriage proposals these past years. For *me* alone. You were supposed to live forever."

"Never got one out of Berenger." There was deliberate cruelty in the taunt.

Darcy came perilously close to cutting her father down. But it could have the profound and damaging effect of snuffing the life out of him. All too often he'd been wrong. Then again it was typical of him to try to catch her out, to goad her into revealing what he was too fearful to face.

"Curt and I would never have worked," she said, holding in the anger she had controlled for years. Outwardly calm, inwardly she was dealing with the old desolation. It was essential she keep a lock on her tongue. She had survived. Her father was dying.

Jock spluttered cruelly. "What the hell do you take me for, girl? You've been hooked on Berenger since you were a kid. Any other woman would have taken him into her bed. I counted on you to resist him." He treated her to a searching stare.

"Don't let's get into this, Dad," she said deciding he hadn't earned the right to her most private thoughts. "It causes too much upset and you can't be upset." Always the placator she feared the onset of another bad turn. "Besides." She gave him what he needed to hear. "I gave my heart to you. You're all I've had." She said it with an enigmatic smile, finally forced to consider all the loving had been on her side.

"Exactly." Jock McIvor nodded, convinced her wholehearted devotion was his due. "As for me, I have no son to take over from me." His breathing hissed with impotent rage. "Just girls. Can you believe it? With my incredible strength.

My virility. The women I've had! I want you to get Berenger over here," he announced with a sudden vigour.

Darcy shook her head in utter confusion. "You want Curt?" Considering the role her father had played in breaking them up this came as a revelation.

"Oh I know we've always had our differences," he grunted, catching sight of her shocked expression. "I know he hasn't any regard for me—glimpses of his old man there—but I've never known a Berenger not to show integrity. Despite all this infernal suffering and pain Doc Robertson tells me I have a little time to go. I want to discuss something with Berenger. Barely thirty and he's building a name for himself," he said grudgingly.

"He's got a name, Dad," Darcy bluntly corrected. "He was born with it. Berenger. A proud name. It's on the record. A name he lives up to. What can you possibly discuss with Curt of *all* people you can't discuss with me?"

"Important business, that's what!" There was a momentary flash in McIvor's eyes. "I know you've got a good head on your shoulders but I need to speak to a man, that man being Curt Berenger."

Darcy's saddened eyes looked steadily into her father's. "Do you love me, Dad?" Please God let him say it just once. "You've never told me. You've said a few times you were proud of me , especially when I won that big endurance race, but love has never been mentioned."

Incredibly a tear trickled from Jock McIvor's eyes. "My fault, Darcy girl. I sometimes think I've never known what real *love* is. Apart from my mother. I'm convinced I loved her. Named you after her, didn't I? I was passionately in love with Marian for a while or at least I thought I was. She was so pretty and amenable. It's possible I loved you girls, I don't know. Maybe loving isn't in my nature. Fidelity either. Now that was beyond me. All I know is I care about *you,* Darcy. You'll be a remarkable woman in later life. By and large you're pretty remarkable now. Your interests will be well protected. You don't have to worry your head about that."

"You're changing your will?" Shock upon shock ground her down.

"Just let's say I'm moving away from the original. I'm on the brink of meeting my Maker. Curiously I've rarely given Him a second thought but now I have a pressing need to straighten things out."

Attonement it seemed was a powerful factor when it came time to die. "You want to include Courtney? I understand that." Courtney who had gone with her mother. Courtney who had abandoned her only sister among other things. Did Courtney deserve to be rewarded? Darcy began to wonder what she had done with her life.

"You're too understanding for your own good," her father gave a rasping cough. "But you've got guts and you got them from me. Get Berenger over here. I'm not that dumb I don't know he'll still do what you ask."

After a long sleepless night battling fresh demons, Darcy drove down to the airstrip midmorning to pick up Curt and deliver him to the homestead. She realized he was putting himself out for her. Curt was a very busy man with many calls on his time and attention. She counted her blessings he remained her friend.

In front of her and to either side, the vast ancient plains spread out as far as the eye could see. Horizon to horizon. The indomitable land under whose influence she had fallen, glowed molten red. She knew without the protection of her sunglasses the fiery sands, ridged like old washboards, would have been blinding to the naked eye. Studded here and there were white boled ghost gums, the pretty little minareechies with their light green leaves and feathery acacias with swarms of little birds, finches and red throats hopping around the branches. Clumps of spinifex, like giant pincushions glinted gold as wheat. Mile after mile of them. A never ending supply of stockfood.

Spinifex and sand. Space, freedom, a million acres to roam. Why wouldn't she love her desert home? In times of severe drought it was like taking a walk on Mars, but all that was forgotten when the heartland blazed into the Garden of Eden after the rains. Today the mirage was working its cruel magic. The desert phenomenon had bedevilled many a past explorer and lost traveller luring them towards what they believed was pure fresh water. Water that shone like a polished mirror. This was the land of mirage. It gave the illusion there was no horizon. Land and sky merged into one.

As she gazed across some of the most starkly beautiful and forbidding land on the planet the speck in the cloudless blue sky swiftly transformed itself into a light aircraft. Darcy swept it with the binoculars that hung around her neck. The Berenger twin-engined Beech Baron. He was right on time.

A few minutes later she watched in admiration as Curt made a perfect touch-down in a brisk cross wind. He taxied up to Murraree's silver hangar, made his after checks then disembarked covering the short distance between them in long loping strides.

One hell of a man was Curt Berenger. Darcy watched his progress with the tense, foolish, feverish, fascination she could never kill off. He was at once daunting and dazzling. Aware of his own power but rarely pressing it. He didn't have to of course. Today, like all other days, she put herself on guard.

"Hi!" He bestowed his beautiful white smile on her. Next best, his dark timbred voice. It had a very attractive edge to it. Sexy was what women called it.

"Hello yourself!" She gave him a light ironic salute. Both of them had perfected the art of taking the mickey out of the other.

At close range he was even more stunning. Emphatically

the cattle baron, a powerful and influential community leader, a target for women. She could never forget. They threw themselves at him. Worshipped at his booted feet. Around Curt Berenger adulation was the order of the day. His classic features were hard planed, damn nearly godlike. He had a firm but full lipped mouth, crystal clear green eyes that positively scintillated in his darkly tanned face. They stared at each other as they always did, way beyond the comfort zone.

She broke first, as ever, tossing her head which meant: *Not me, Curt. Never again.*

"Thanks so much for coming," she said briskly, conscious she was *breathing* him in.

He started to walk with her to the jeep, adjusting his broad brimmed akubra over his eyes. "Given the brutal fact your dad and I have never got on—and we both know why—this is downright weird."

Forbidden topic. "I agree but he trusts you."

"Does he really?" Curt treated her to a sarcastic stare.

"It's something to do with a new will," she explained.

"Wha-a-t!" Curt did a double take.

"You heard me." Tall as she was she had to tilt her head to look up at him. Something she found very satisfying.

"Hell, Darcy." He registered his disgust. "Even now he's playing with your emotions. What prompted this I wonder? And why *me?* It's not making a lot of sense." He didn't wait to be invited, he slid behind the wheel of the jeep.

"People see things in a different way when they're dying." Darcy settled herself in the passenger side without comment. She was long used to Curt's ways. "Whatever our history, underneath he respects you as a Berenger."

"Does he, the old…so and so," Curt swallowed on what he really wanted to call Jock McIvor. "Does he mean to include Courtney?" He put the jeep into gear, heading for the long unsealed track that led to the main compound.

"She *is* his daughter." Darcy clamped her hands together. It was an automatic response to Curt's closeness.

"She's fairly well ignored that up-to-date. I wonder what he's up to? For all his periodic bursts of charm your father is an unpredictable and ruthless man." People's view of Darcy was that she was a *saint* for putting up with her notoriously difficult father let alone loving him. But such was the parental bond. McIvor represented all Darcy knew since her mother had opted out at an age when Darcy had desperately needed her.

"I don't really know what's going on in his head," Darcy said, pursing her lips in thought. "I don't think I've ever known. As for Courtney, maybe she felt she'd be as unwanted here as I'd be unwanted there. My mother obviously decided she wanted nothing more to do with us." She didn't dare mention to Curt her father's stunning confession her mother had wanted her to attend her second wedding. That would only give him more ammunition. Maybe there were more secrets in store for her? After all, didn't she have her own?

"Probably it was all so painful she had to break the connection just to survive," Curt looked into her eyes briefly. "Your mother needed love and admiration like the rest of us. She didn't get it from your dear father. The thing that has always surprised me was your father didn't let her have custody of both of you if only because of his lifestyle. He could have had you for the holidays. A compassionate man wouldn't force such a traumatic separation. Children generally stay with their mother."

"You seem to be forgetting. My mother didn't want me. At least Dad *did*." Darcy kept the pain and anger out of her voice. She was done with self-pity.

"That's the line your father sold you. He drummed it into you from Day One. You were twelve years old. The unimaginable had happened. Your father was so desperate to hold onto you he shifted all the blame onto your mother. My mother insists to this day your mother adored you. You know that."

"Strange way of showing it," Darcy answered crisply. "Kath is just being Kath offering comfort."

"Not only that," Curt insisted. "Mum's very fond of you of course, but she's always been convinced your father had something on your mother he used as leverage. Or it was plain spite. You know what's he like. She couldn't have both of you. Come on, Darcy, your mother was a gentle, loving person. It must have been horrible for her. She wasn't suited to station life but she tried for a long time. Your father was a big intimidating man. He made his wife suffer."

"You mean with the affairs?" Darcy stared out at the sun scorched landscape, deriving comfort from its rugged grandeur. How she had hated it when her father had occasionally brought his girlfriends home. Though in all fairness most had tried to be kind to her.

"It must have been a tremendous threat to her self-esteem thus to the marriage."

"He must have needed something she couldn't give him," Darcy sighed. "Sex was a very important part of Dad's life. He couldn't live without it."

"Unlike *you,*" he said in a bone dry voice.

"Well, you could never lead a celibate life," she retorted, turning her head away.

"What the hell are you talking about?" He picked up on that quickly. "I don't know what fool image of me you've got in your head, but it's certainly not based on reality. I am not your father, Darcy. How can you think that for a minute?"

She dug her nails into her palms. "Whenever you take your trips to the big cities I'm sure you don't move around alone." She had the proof. She had never spoken it aloud.

"Why because sometimes I get my picture in the paper?" he challenged.

Oh yes, she thought. You get your picture taken. "Let's

move off the subject," she said. "I'm sorry I started it. Just say you're very macho. Our way of life promotes it."

"For goodness' sake, Darcy!" Curt grunted. "I swear I don't know what you're on about some times. I suppose you can't help it given the life you've led. I admit men are in control out here, if that's what you call macho. Men determine the industry. As for your father, sex for him must have been like his drinking. An appetite. Maybe a form of recreation. Think about it. Was anyone really special to him? I know this is one hell of an explosive issue between us, but you're forever locked into making excuses for your dad. It's become second nature. I can't believe he has ever really loved anyone in his entire life."

It was a claim she desperately wanted to deny, but it was probably true. Darcy lifted her eyes to a squadron of budgerigars that flew in emerald and gold formation alongside the speeding vehicle. It was one of the great sights of her homeland. "Dad said he loved his mother," she offered quietly.

"Well that's *one* person," Curt's mouth tilted at the corners with dark humour. "I'm not saying he doesn't care about you, Darcy. You're his prize possession. The one that didn't get away. I understand your allegiance even if it drives me nuts. You've only had him to turn to at a crucial time of your life. Every young girl needs her mother."

"To develop right?" She was aware she had been severely damaged by her mother's abandonment.

"Absolutely! Your dad even if he'd been a loving dad couldn't have taken over that role. Darcy, he treated you—mistreated you if you like—like a boy. The son he never had. You give him everything. What does he give to you? Now a new will. What does that mean? Could it put your interests at risk in some way? Your interests must be protected. Maybe his choice of daughter goes back to the fact you're said to resemble his mother. The mystical bond, perhaps?"

"Go to hell," she said quietly.

"I'm trying to live my life to make certain I won't," he clipped off. "Your father was prepared to let Courtney go. He couldn't keep your mother against her will but you were the one he wanted. You were the one he *needed.* Even at twelve you were brave, resourceful, competent, loyal. You loved the land when your mother and sister didn't. You were fearless. You stood out and Courtney was a babe in arms beside you. She wasn't a physical child in the sense you were. There was her fear of horses. Your father was to blame for that with his bluster and bullying. Instead of using a gentle hand he seemed to go out of his way to frighten her. They just didn't come more rambunctious than your old man."

"Rambunctious?" She gave a bitter little smile. "That's a good word. He's not so rambunctious now."

Curt eyed her purely cut profile, the small straight nose, the delicately determined chin, the swan's neck. Her lustrous mane of sable hair hung down her back in a thick plait. Her olive skin glowed with good health. No make-up save the usual token touch of lipstick. She was beautiful and ludicrously unaware of it. Inevitable perhaps when her father made a point of ignoring her feminine attractiveness. "I'm sorry, Darcy," he said gently, and he *was,* though sometimes he wanted to shake the living daylights out of her. "I know what your father means to you. We're predisposed to love our parents no matter what. What I don't know is what he wants with me now? Given he's done everything in his power to drive a wedge between us it's damned odd. I don't want to be put into the position of advising on wills. He has a team of lawyers for that. Maxwell and Maynard. Adam Maynard is a man of integrity with a fine legal brain. Your father has spoken to Adam hasn't he?"

She pulled a face. "You know Dad never took to Adam any more than Adam took to Dad."

"Your father isn't an easy man to like."

"How unkind." She bit her lip.

"The unvarnished truth. Lots of people have been taken in by Jock. Women in particular. Some women will always be attracted to dangerous men."

"You're pretty dangerous yourself." Her profound feelings for him spilled over, as on rare occasions they did.

His green eyes sought hers. "Rubbish!" His tone was a mix of disgust and wry humour. "I'm just a pussy cat."

"A jaguar." She didn't smile. "We'll never see eye to eye, Curt."

He turned his head. "That wouldn't stand up to examination. What about the land which we love more than anything else. The land and everything that goes with it. Then there's our love of horses and horsemanship, of books and music. We share the same sense of humour. We like the same people. Our political leanings are the same, our world view. Apart from that we don't have a darn thing in common. I agree. There's quite a gap."

Jock McIvor had foregone his medication so his mind would be clear. With difficulty he lifted his head as his daughter and Curt Berenger were shown into his bedroom by the incredibly dull and dour Ainsworth woman. Berenger stood inches over the head of his tall daughter, making her look darn near fragile. Funny he had never thought of Darcy as being fragile before. Darcy could handle rough work with the best of them.

"Good of you to come, Curt." It came out in a hoarse bark.

Berenger inclined his handsome head.

As arrogant as his father McIvor thought, but it was the arrogance of achievement.

"Anything I can do to help *Darcy,* sir," Curt said formally, moving to the bedside to take the withered hand that was extended to him. Curt recalled how big and powerful that hand had once been.

He was shocked by the deterioration in McIvor's condition. McIvor looked very close to death. That inevitably stirred feelings of pity. However devious and demanding, Jock McIvor had been a giant of a man. To be reduced to this wasted hulk! It was cruel. Terminal illness was a down-casting fact of life.

"You don't need to stay, Darcy," McIvor rasped. "I need to talk to Curt alone."

"Surely there's nothing Darcy can't hear?" Curt questioned, looking briefly over his shoulder towards Darcy. He hoped she'd insist on staying but her father had such a hold on her.

Darcy returned Curt's challenging green gaze briefly then dipped her head. "I'll go see about lunch. You're staying, Curt?"

He nodded. "Don't go to any trouble. Make it simple."

"See you later then." Darcy turned and moved quietly out of the room.

"Don't like me much do you, Curt?" McIvor rubbed a hand still rough with a lifetime's callouses against the smooth sheet.

Understatement of the year. "You've never done anything to make me like you, Jock. Then I don't think it has ever mattered to you if you were liked or not. " Curt brought up a chair to the bed.

"Your dad didn't care for me either. I suspect your parents thought I was responsible for Marian's running off?"

"Were you?" Curt asked bluntly.

McIvor's frown was fierce. "She threatened to destroy me if I didn't let her go."

"How could she do that?" Curt struggled to understand.

"She knew where the bodies were buried."

"I didn't know she played any role in your business affairs?" It was well known McIvor barely recognised women outside their sexual desirability.

"She didn't play any role," he huffed. "Didn't have a brain in her fluffy blonde head. Like all women."

"That's not true, Jock," Curt said. He wasn't about to start an argument with a desperately ill man. "Women just didn't get the opportunities. They were kept busy raising children. Anyway your own daughter gives the lie to that. Darcy's had increasing input into the station affairs. I'd trust her anytime."

"That's because I trained her." McIvor coughed and tried to get his breath back. "But she's a woman. Women are weak, vulnerable. They're putty in a man's hands."

"No way does that apply to Darcy." Curt fixed his eyes steadily on McIvor's. "She knows how to take care of herself."

"That's because *I'm* around." McIvor, the confirmed chauvinist, was convinced of it. "What about when I'm not? I've got a lot to leave, my boy. I've looked after my affairs so well. Darcy will sure as hell be a mark as an heiress."

"Perhaps she will but she can handle it," Curt returned confidently.

"You sure about that? Life's a bloody jungle. She's been protected so far. The two of you have grown up together. I know you've got strong feelings for her."

"Which you did your best to crush," Curt didn't hesitate to say. "You've been absolutely against Darcy and me but it's much too late to talk about it now. What were you about to suggest, Jock? We do a complete about face? I marry Darcy to protect the most important thing in the world to you? We all know what that is. Murraree. Only neither Darcy nor I could be bought out."

"It might turn out that way all the same," McIvor was moved to predict, his bitter expression betraying he was not entirely coming to terms with it even when he was dying.

"Why don't you cut to the chase, Jock," Curt suggested, feeling like getting up and walking away. "What have you really got me here for?"

McIvor gave a dry cough, trying to ignore the pain over which he had no control. "Now, now, remember I'm a sick man. No matter what you *say,* you make it your business to look out for Darcy."

Curt admitted as much with an abrupt nod of his head.

"She must be protected." McIvor gave another harsh cough. He stared past Curt's mahogany head to the portrait across the room. "I have to settle my life, son. Do you understand that?"

"Of course I do." Curt was straightforward with his answer. "I understand from Darcy you now wish to consider Courtney?"

McIvor swallowed on a throat that was perpetually parched. "Some women find it the simplest thing to give a man sons. Others can only manage giving a man in my position daughters."

"Hang on, Jock, are you sure of that?" Curt pressed.

"Don't listen to rumours, son. They're not true. I have no son, a curse which even now when I'm dying I can't adjust to. Your dad was the lucky one."

"My dad lost his life prematurely." Curt commented sombrely, still grieving for the father he idolized.

"I know and I'm sorry but he had *you.* He had an heir to take over the reins." McIvor's grey face was thwarted and angry.

"You have Darcy," Curt answered him. "Tom McLaren is a good manager. Darcy has friends. She's much admired in the community."

"Course she is, but she's a woman. Running a big cattle station is a man's job. It's endless back breaking work. You know that. Then she'd have to cope with the men. They behave when I'm around, but there are those that eye her off. I see 'em. If they ever went near her I'd shoot 'em. Darcy is an Outback woman to the core. She loves the land like we do. She's the eldest, the first born. She'll get the lion's share."

"I should hope so. She deserves it," Curt looked closely at the dying man. McIvor was *so* unpredictable.

"Always on her side," McIvor snorted. "It's a bizarre relationship you two have. I almost regret now the things I've done."

Curt almost laughed aloud. "I've always blamed you, Jock. Make no mistake about that. But to get back to why I'm here. You want to draw up a new document recognizing Courtney? Is that it?"

"Yes." A shudder shook McIvor's wasted frame.

"Are you all right? Clearly you're in a lot of pain." Curt half stood up.

"Maybe a drink of water."

Curt poured it, assisting McIvor to drink. "I was thinking of a trust fund," McIvor managed eventually when he was resting back on the pillows. "I want you to play a part in that. Trustee now your dad's gone. I would have asked him."

"Jock! Do you want to give Darcy another reason to resent me?" Curt groaned. "She can handle her own affairs."

McIvor looked back with genuine scorn. "In my judgment it would be best if a man like you kept a careful eye on things."

"There are good reliable responsible professionals who could do that." Curt argued. "Your solicitors Maxwell & Maynard. You should be discussing this all important issue with them. I would have thought time was critical."

McIvor frowned. "I wanted to talk to you first. No matter what you think of me—what I've done—and I admit I took every opportunity to cause trouble—I trust you. Besides you Berengers have more than enough money and property of your own. Maybe things between you and Darcy went sour but I'll stake my life—what's left of it—you'll look out for her."

Curt's expression was not encouraging. "Why didn't you discuss this with Adam Maynard when he was last here?"

McIvor beetled his brows. "He's not a favourite of mine. He's not one of *us*. You're the man I trust. You're a cattle man just like me and you're familiar with the whole situation. Darcy needs you as an adviser, a man who can help her plan for the future. I don't want to see all us McIvors have worked for go down the drain."

"That I understand." Curt nodded his agreement. "But let me get Darcy in here, Jock. You wanted my advice. That's it. Get her in here. Don't leave her in the dark. She's not a child. She's a responsible adult."

McIvor pressed back against the pillows. "I can't handle it," he barked, looking pathetically ill. "Darcy being Darcy will launch into one of her little tirades. Don't think she's not above telling her own father off. I'm not saying she doesn't have the business acumen to handle the McIvor fortune if it weren't for the fact she's a *woman*. You know as well as I do men stalk women with money."

Curt knew better than most inheriting a fortune was a heavy responsibility. "So you figure setting up a family trust will protect Darcy and presumably Courtney?"

"Who's probably a complete ninny like her mother and just as beautiful. There'll be plenty of men around to exploit her. Mark my words! There's marriage, divorce. These things happen. Hell, I should know. Some bloody con man could go off with my money. No wonder there are prenuptial agreements. It's the only way to go."

Curt forced himself to sound as calm as possible. "So Darcy and Courtney are the main beneficiaries?" He wondered if there weren't somebody else in the woodwork given McIvor's numerous liasons.

McIvor cleared his throat several times. "Yes," he managed hoarsely.

"The trust administers the estate and apportions income to your daughters. You'd have to decide how much."

"They'll have enough!" McIvor muttered irritably.

"I think you should line up another couple of trustees," Curt suggested.

"Okay, okay." McIvor waved a withered hand. "I'm telling you Curt it's the only way I'll die happy. I need a man of impeccable reputation who has more than enough interests of his own to act as the main trustee and executor of my estate. I believe I've come up with the right man. *You.* And if you won't do it I'll have to get someone else," he added with grim determination. "Someone who mightn't always act in the best interests of the beneficiaries."

That forced Curt to reconsider. McIvor's expression told him he meant exactly what he said. "Jock, you're putting a lot on me. Darcy won't like this idea."

"It's not Darcy's money!" McIvor glared, his voice suddenly strong. "Murraree belongs to *me.* If she wants to make trouble she mightn't be named as a beneficiary at all. Now I'm tired," he announced gruffly. "Get that dratted Ainsworth woman in here, will you? She's plain, poor bitch. No woman should be as plain as that and she stinks of disinfectant. I don't want to hurt Darcy but I won't tolerate any stubbornness. Explain that to her."

CHAPTER TWO

CURT left McIvor's bedroom feeling like he was wading through quick sand. The nurse was hovering nearby and he lost no time telling her Mr. McIvor was in need of his medication. He then went in search of Darcy, finding her in the kitchen, washing a head of lettuce at the sink.

"Ham and salad okay?" she asked in a way that suggested her mind wasn't on fixing lunch at all.

"Fine." His voice too came out more clipped than he intended. "Make it a sandwich and a cup of coffee, Darcy. I have to talk to you."

"Of course you do and from the expression on your face you know I won't like it. Dad is selling Murraree to you. At the right price, of course." Although she was joking Darcy's golden skin had turned pale. Anything was possible with her father.

Curt gave a harsh laugh. He pulled out a chair and sat down. "That'd be one for the books!" The kitchen was enormous and very old-fashioned. Like the rest of the rambling old homestead it was badly in need of updating and refurbishing. For all his money McIvor was notoriously tight fisted. "Let's make this clear. I don't want Murraree, Darcy," he said, aware of her loss of colour. "I have enough on my hands."

She shook her gleaming head. "You wouldn't knock it back if it came on the market?"

"I'm not getting into any hypothetical discussions. Come here and sit down."

"I'll make you a sandwich first. The coffee will only take a minute. I'll put it on the stove." For a few moments neither spoke as she worked quickly putting together a plate of ham and salad sandwiches. "So what did Dad suggest?" she asked finally, setting the plate before him along with a clean white linen napkin.

"This looks good," he said, realizing he was hungry. He hadn't eaten since dawn. "You're going to have something surely?" He looked up at her.

"I seem to have lost my appetite."

"You can't afford to. You're downright skinny." The expression in his green eyes changed, as they travelled over her.

Sometimes he slipped back into doing that so the blood raced through her veins. "Why do you do it, Curt?" she asked, thoroughly rattled.

"Call you skinny?" he half smiled.

"You know darn well. Look at me like that?"

He sat back, considering. "Well apart from being skinny you're just beautiful even with a pigtail hanging down your back. I can't remember the last time I saw your hair out."

"You do too," she reminded him shortly. "The last polo ball."

"That's right. Damn near a year ago. Sunset hosts it this time around. I remember you spent most of the night with Rob Erskine," he referred to a member of his team who had always been painfully in love with Darcy and unbeknown to him had actually proposed to her.

"So I did." She shrugged. "While you gave Beth Gilmour the best night of her life. Both of them now out of the picture."

"Oh yeah?" he mocked. "I saw Beth only the other day."

"Actually she'd make you a good wife."

Curt gave her a disgusted look. "We've been through this

before, Darcy. I'm allergic to having a wife picked out for me by *you!*"

The tantalizing aroma of perking coffee filled the kitchen. "You always taunt me about my single state. Why can't I have a go at you?"

"Taunt away," he invited, waving a careless hand. "You, my dear Darcy, are an open book. You want a review? It's as I always tell you. You're terrified of giving your heart away. You construct defences that make you feel safe, presumably against loss. Unfortunately loss is inevitable in life. You've been a victim. That's why you're compelled to act as you do."

"You should have taken up psychiatry." She raked an escaped lock of hair off her face.

He shrugged. "Anyone could see your conflicts."

"Loving *you* a woman could get hurt badly." She risked a glance at him, determined to keep her sensual self closed off when obviously she couldn't.

"A woman meaning *you.* Don't sound so miserable. Eventually you'll work it out. I just hope you don't leave it until your child bearing years are over. I think you'd make a great mother. I see you when you're around little kids, teenagers come to that. Remember those so called problem kids we took on at Sunset last year? They thought you were great. You handled them so well. Firm but gentle, ready to listen, encouraging them. You interacted better than anyone else. Including my mother. I recall an eternity ago I had high hopes for us."

For a few seconds she had difficulty continuing with what she was doing. Her hands shook. "I wouldn't have been good for you, Curt. Nor you for me. We'd have ruined each other's lives by now. I thought we'd established that." Once she and Curt had been lovers—one of those great desperate romances that ended very badly. There was danger in even stirring over the ashes.

Determinedly she switched the conversation. "So what did Dad say?"

The corners of Curt's firm mouth turned down. "That's right, change the subject. I messed up, didn't I? I should have made allowances for your insecurities instead I frightened you away. Maybe you saw it as self-preservation. But Darcy, I thought you were ripe for loving."

She sought sanctuary at the kitchen sink. "Was I wrong or did we take our loving to extremes? If you'd asked me to run off to the other side of the world with you I would have. Then what would have happened to Dad? It was bad enough trying to keep all my feelings locked away despite having plenty of experience."

"Don't you realise the fact you felt compelled to lock your feelings away indicates a serious problem," Curt asked with a hint of severity. "Your father has been the cause of much unhappiness, Darcy. I think you provide the clearest illustration."

The truth of that gripped her. "Please, Curt, let it go. It's all ancient history anyway. I might look tough but underneath I'm mighty vulnerable."

"You're telling *me?* You project your mother's problems on to yourself. As far as looking tough? You might be a fighter, Darcy, but look tough, you *don't.* I've had so much time to consider. You ran from me because you felt threatened. Is that it? You never attempted to explain. Poor mug me, was on top of the world. I just floated through life then, on Cloud Nine. I know you were frightened of your own sex drive let alone mine. Anyone would think our lovemaking had corrupted you."

She could never forget the intensity. "It was incredibly passionate." She lowered her head, not allowing him to see her eyes. "Maybe I thought your idea of me wasn't the *real* me. How could you have professed to love me so much? You could have had anyone. All the blue-blooded society girls. Not tormented old me. I was paralysed by the fear you'd eventually cast me aside and I needed to get out before then. Maybe what you're saying is true. I can't differentiate between myself and my mother. What happened between us got way out of control. Isn't the word passion derived from the Greek *penthos* to grieve? Strong passions can cause suffering."

"So your answer was to escape? I never knew you were such a coward."

"There's lots you don't know," she said, suddenly wanting to run. "How could I cope with being Curt Berenger's *wife?* Now that's a big job. Who knows some time down the track I could be sent packing."

He put his hands flat on the table and stared at her. "It all comes back to your own family. I don't care to be lumped in with your father."

Darcy shook her head. "Aren't you both alpha males?"

He reacted vehemently to that. "The only similarity is we're both cattle men, extraordinarily successful at what we do. In your father's case, *did.* I do *not* have a callous hand with women. I am not a womaniser despite your quite insulting ideas. I am not bloody mean and shockingly selfish and I'm fairly certain I don't have the reputation for being a bastard. I'm intelligent, good natured and dare I say it, attractive. You're the only woman I know who goes into panic mode at the very sight of me. Don't bother denying it. I can see through the smoke screen."

"Maybe you can," she expressed a sigh. "But what's in it for us, Curt, but high risk? For a while there you had me body and soul. It's something I can't allow."

"Fearless in so many ways, timid in others," he accused.

Darcy shook her head. "*You* say timid. *I* say keeping myself together."

"You won't stay together long with all this hard physical labour," Curt retorted. "And for goodness' sake, sit down." He waited until she did before resuming. "What you do is much too hard for a woman though your father has allowed it. It has to stop. It *will* stop."

Colour stained her high cheekbones. "You mean when *you* take over? Are you trying to tell me it's a possibility?"

He looked angry at the question and the deep resentment in her tone. "I don't have to tell you running a cattle station involves excessive hard work seven days a week. I don't know how you've been able to keep it up but it can't last. It will steal your youth and your strength. You need help Darcy. What's more, you're going to get it."

"Dad has elected you the new Boss." She brought out bitterness like a weapon.

"Give me a break, Darcy." They were at it again. "I'm not going to ruin things for you. I'm going to help you."

"Wouldn't I be lost without you?" She was becoming increasingly angry and confused.

"Well we're sitting here together, aren't we?" he shot back.

"So it seems." Darcy tried to get a rein on herself but the pressure was too much. "Would you like another cup of coffee?" she asked bleakly.

"Please. It's excellent." He presented his empty cup, thinking what he was saying was having little effect.

"You were the one who brought the beans back from the city for me," Darcy reminded him, refilling their cups. "So let it out. What have you got to say that's going to surprise me?"

Curt didn't beat about the bush. "You know your father's views. He is without question a chauvinist."

"Yes," she answered sharply, betraying her worry over what was coming.

"In the original will you were the sole beneficiary apart from a few minor bequests."

"I know."

"You were right in thinking your father wants to acknowledge Courtney."

Darcy sighed deeply. "She is his daughter. I have no real problem with that providing she has no say in running Murraree about which she knows nothing."

"Your father wants to set up a trust fund." Curt took a long swallow of the hot steaming coffee and set down the cup.

Darcy's aquamarine eyes flashed. "A trust fund. C'mon?" she jeered.

"He doesn't think you could run Murraree by yourself. You can't, without help. I know you're that realistic. His big concern, however, is you and Courtney will become targets for unscrupulous suitors."

"So he wants to set up a trust fund with *you* the trustee?" Darcy looked angry, contemptuous and humiliated all at the same time. "I knew it. He wants you to run the bloody place."

"I knew *exactly* your reaction." He too gave way to anger.

"When you come right down to it, who else?" She shoved her plate away. "You're the right man for the job."

"You mean I'm the last person you'd *want* in the job?" He leaned a fraction closer tall and rangy with those wide shoulders. "The last man you'd *want.*"

"Why should I have you or anyone?" she demanded to know.

"Because you need someone better than Tom McLaren, your present manager," Curt ground out. "Tom's a good man, experienced at what he does, but he can't take control, much less do your father's job. It's your father's station and it's your father's money. You'll be a rich woman when he dies. Better yet, a *free* woman. So will Courtney. Though as I understand it you'll have the lion's share."

"I should bloody hope so," she swore again without apology. "I can imagine Courtney will be thrilled. She'll probably decide to come out here to inspect her property. She might even bring my mother and her second husband. After all, they'd have nothing to fear anymore. Dad will be gone. How does this trust fund work?" Her slanting eyes with their winged black brows glittered her anger was so apparent.

"The usual way. The trustees, probably three, two from Maxwell-Maynard—"

"Adam?" she interrupted.

"He'd be a good choice."

"You being in charge of course. You're the man to take control."

He gave her a look of total exasperation. "This wasn't my idea."

"I wonder?"

His handsome features tightened into severity. "Don't be ridiculous," he said sharply. "I expect an apology."

"Okay. I apologise." Her voice was so brittle it crackled. "I wasn't thinking about your splendid ethics. Correct me if I'm wrong. *You* hold the reins. *You* make the decisions. *You* decide what Courtney and I as beneficiaries get. I have to go to you cap in hand whenever I want something in relation to the running of the station." As she spoke she shoved back her chair and stood up, beginning to pace about the kitchen

Curt was unsurprised by her anger. He studied her willowy figure clad in its everyday garb of tight fitting jeans and T-shirt. Today it was a bright scarlet T-shirt that suited her complexion, the manufacturer's logo stitched across the front in navy. She had small, but beautifully shaped breasts, just the right butt and long legs for jeans. The kind of body that made riding gear look damn near *haute couture*. "Take pity on me. I'm not spoiling for a fight."

"Well I am," she said fierily. "Murraree is none of your business."

"If you were a horse you'd have your ears flat against your head and you'd be baring your teeth. As usual, you're not thinking about *me*. Why should I want more work? The fact of the matter is, if your father doesn't appoint me he'll find someone else. He told me so in no uncertain terms. That's what swayed me. Do you *want* someone else? All I'm going to be, Darcy, is a guiding hand. A friend. Nothing more."

"It's an outrage. It's awful," Darcy cried.

"Don't look so martyred. You're not being thrown off."

Darcy ignored him. "I am an experienced, responsible woman, not an idiot. I grew up on a cattle station unlike Courtney who doesn't know a thing about it."

"Spare yourself a lot of grief, Darcy," Curt advised her. "Don't fight your father on this. He's determined on taking this course. His aim however much you disagree is to protect his fortune. Courtney mightn't be as level-headed as you."

"This document doesn't even exist," Darcy said hopefully.

"No, but Jock wants the lawyers back."

"He could die at any time," Darcy looked skyward. As if her father had already taken off on wings.

Curt sighed. "I'll bet whatever you like he survives until after a carefully prepared will is drawn up."

"I could argue he wasn't of sound mind."

"I doubt you'd get anyone to agree with you. I didn't fly over here this morning to do your father's bidding and in doing so anger you. Jock is set on his course. He has a perfect right to do whatever he wants with his money. And with Murraree. It's a wonder he doesn't want it sold up after he's gone. He's of the opinion he's the last of the line. No woman could run the station on her own. It's killing work. Your husband according to Jock might well be a waster."

Reluctantly Darcy returned to her chair, a wash of tears over her eyes. "Maybe the reason for this decision is Dad is now reconciled to the notion I might end up marrying you?"

"Better the devil you know than the devil you don't," Curt said with a flash of contempt. "However, for all my unbridled lust which so frightened you, I never got around to asking you to marry me though I went to the city to buy you an engagement ring. Don't look so shocked. Some fiancée you'd have made never trusting me. These days there are just too many suitable girls around *without* your problems and unresolved conflicts. But at a professional level I think we could work together very well."

She blinked furiously, fighting the impulse to do something—*anything*—to relieve the intense pressure his admission had put on her. An engagement ring? My God! "I'm dead against this," she said.

"Tell your father." Curt was acutely aware of her sense of betrayal. "That's if you're prepared to thoroughly antagonise him. I hardly think Jock McIvor is the man to change his mind once it's made up."

CHAPTER THREE

IN THE middle of the broad flight of stone steps leading up to the homestead's verandah, stood a small graceful figure.

Her sister.

A few feet behind her, impressively tall and elegant, Adam Maynard, the solicitor, his dark hair in the sunlight glossy as a crow's wing. Adam had arranged the charter flight from Brisbane. He would be staying a few days. The young woman, enchantingly pretty, moved forward blindly. Tears flowed from her large azure blue eyes.

"Darcy!"

Darcy's heart gave a great jolt that wasn't apparent from her sober expression. It wasn't hard to reconcile this lovely apparition with the image of the ten-year-old-girl Darcy carried in her head. Her sister, Courtney, was still the image of their mother.

Darcy put out her hand. "So you finally got here, Courtney?"

Courtney ignored the outstretched hand and the cool, regal demeanour. As a little girl she had adored her big sister. She ran up the steps and hugged her sister hard. "Oh, Darcy! Oh, Darcy!" she cried, like she had been drowning and Darcy was her saviour.

Though it cost her the greatest effort for she too was in a highly emotional state, Darcy remained enormously guarded. She gazed over her sister's blonde head—she couldn't have been more than five-two—at the lawyer. "How are you, Adam?"

"Fine, thanks, Darcy. And you?"

"A bit shaky. Dad's life is hanging by a thread."

"It must be very difficult for you, Darcy," Adam said, feeling an uprush of sympathy for this gutsy young woman whom he had come to admire. At the best of times he found Jock McIvor a devious, controlling sort of man but clearly Darcy loved him so there had to be some good in him.

Adam stood there, allowed his perceptive dark eyes to record the momentous meeting of those two young women parted for so long. Physically they couldn't have been more different. Darcy, taller than most women, slim as a reed, athletic, long shining dark hair pulled back in the familiar thick plait and those incredible slanting aquamarine eyes; her younger sister Courtney her blue eyes huge with tears as adorable as a Persian kitten with all a kitten's cuddly charm. She should have been intimidated by her older sister's manner—Darcy was on her home ground—but there wasn't the slightest awkwardness about her. She appeared genuinely overcome by emotion, thrilled to be reunited with her sister.

It could, however, be an act, Adam found himself thinking cynically. He had seen a lot of duplicitous behaviour over the past years. Especially from the beneficiaries of wills. Remarkably Jock McIvor still clung to life, claiming he wouldn't shut his eyes forever until he had seen his daughter, Courtney once more. This could be Courtney's big chance to effect a highly rewarding reconciliation.

"Come in," Darcy invited, extending her arm. She might as well have added, since you're here. She glanced at her watch. "Curt is flying in. He should be here soon. There are matters he wants to discuss with you, Adam, I understand?"

"We do have things to discuss," Adam confirmed looking back over his shoulder towards the jeep. A station hand had been detailed to drive them up to the homestead from the airstrip. Now this man with the bow legs of someone scarcely ever out of the saddle, was setting several pieces of luggage on the circular drive.

"Don't worry about your things, Adam," Darcy said. "Gordon will bring the luggage up to your rooms." Darcy's eyes touched on her sister briefly when she really wanted to stare and stare, familiarize herself with Courtney the adult. "Dad is anxious to see you the moment you arrive, Courtney. I expect you'd like to freshen up first?" She already looked as fresh as a newly sprung flower.

"Thank you, Darcy. My heart is pounding." Courtney stared tentatively into the shadowy cool of the house. "I can't believe I'm here. It's like the recurrent dream I had for years. I still have it from time to time. But this is *reality!*"

For a fraction of a second Darcy felt like bursting into tears but she'd been too well trained. It would take quite a while for her to re-trust her sister again. "How many years is it?"

"An eternity," Courtney replied, impetuously sliding her hand into her sister's. Just like the old days, Darcy thought, stiffening against the warm soft pressure. "I've missed you all my life."

Darcy needed all her strength to resist that gentle grasp. "You handled it," she pointed out in a dry tone. "So what was the big problem? Did your mother forbid you to come out here? She might have been able to when you were a child. But you're twenty-four."

"All that wasted time," Courtney acknowledged the resistance in her sister's hand by letting it go. "The answer is simple, Darcy. Our father didn't want me here. He made that very, very, plain."

"Really? Haven't times changed."

"At the end people do change, Darcy," Courtney said quietly. "The prospect of death is bigger than even Jock McIvor it seems. He must want to make amends."

"It would seem so." There was no bitterness in the way

Darcy said it. In truth, though she was at great pains to hide it, she was trembling with emotion inside. Her little sister was lovely, immensely graceful, feminine in a way she could never be. Courtney wore a very chic white ruffled shirt with little insets of cotton lace and turquoise detail, turquoise cotton jeans with a pretty belt slung around her tiny waist. Her hair was cut medium short and brushed into a sunburst of curls around her small featured face. Her expression was as sweet as Darcy remembered. There was a purity about her that was extremely engaging.

Yet her sister had betrayed her, Darcy reminded herself. Who wouldn't come running when they were offered a few million dollars?

"This is beautiful! You've gone to a lot of trouble." Courtney wandered in a kind of dream around what had been her mother's bedroom. Her parents had never shared the master suite. That had been their father's exclusively not that their mother had been relegated to a lesser suite. Although this bedroom wasn't as huge as the master bedroom it shared the same splendid view of the home grounds with the magnificent pink lady waterlily lagoon. It was filled with a collection of French furniture and many beautiful things that to Courtney's dazzled eyes had never been moved since her mother's time.

Sunlight streamed in from the verandah across the Aubusson rug, the soft silks and brocades, the Louis chairs, the pink roses in a porcelain vase.

"You've never used this room?" Courtney asked her sister gently.

"Why would I?" Darcy returned more sharply than she intended. It was because inside she was so upset. "I had to try to forget I had a mother. It was hard work."

"Mum wasn't the villain, Darcy." Courtney hung her head. "She left here in despair. We both did."

"You *left* though, didn't you?" Darcy went on the attack. "You didn't take me with you."

"Don't you think we paid for it?" Courtney moaned softly. "Dad was a dangerous man. Surely you'll allow that? Mum was very fearful of him."

"So how did she manage to get away? Not on her own, either. With *you!*"

The tears weren't far from Courtney's eyes. She couldn't get over how beautiful her sister was. And how *angry.* "Mum told me right from the start she was only allowed to take one of us."

"Naturally it was you," Darcy said in a deeply disturbed voice. "The ten year old version of her mother."

"Dad made the choice for her." Courtney whispered it, as though it was too painful to be said out loud.

Darcy's gem coloured eyes flashed. "I don't believe that."

"I believe Mum." Courtney shook her golden head. "She was scared of him, Darcy. I remember he used to take out his temper on her. You must remember too, because you were the one who risked sticking up for her. Lots of people were scared of him. You saw him through different eyes. You could do all the things I couldn't do. You were the one Dad wanted. Make no mistake about it."

"That's what your mother wanted you to believe." Darcy lifted a shaky hand to rub at her temple. It wasn't the time now to lose all faith in her father.

"She's *your* mother too, Darcy." Courtney reminded her.

"She's a hard, uncaring woman!" Darcy said in ringing tones. "She threw me away like a rag doll when I most needed her."

Courtney gave a profound sigh. "Mum must have been desperately unhappy in her marriage. We were too young to understand. Dad ruined life for her. She was in an awful situation. She believed she could get away with the two of us but Dad is a vengeful man. He must have convinced her he'd destroy her if she didn't leave you behind."

Darcy laughed that to scorn. "What was she so afraid of? He couldn't commit murder."

"Who knows what he had in mind," Courtney said, obviously believing anything to be true. "I was a child, Darcy. Younger than you. I didn't understand anything. I'd done nothing wrong."

"Neither had I." All these years she had borne the scars. Courtney, at least, had had the loving comfort of their mother. The gentleness, the female tenderness and sharing. Whatever her deep feelings for her father Darcy knew she hadn't had that.

Courtney was unashamedly crying. "Mum lost the battle, Darcy. She was right to be afraid."

"So afraid she left *me* in the firing line," Darcy countered passionately. "Why did she let you come out here *now?*"

Courtney took a tissue from her pocket and blew her nose, as Darcy expected, daintily. "She could hardly stop me. I live my own life. I share an apartment with a girlfriend, but I see Mum and Peter all the time. Mum didn't want me to come. She tore up the letter the solicitor sent me. She didn't want me to have anything to do with Dad even when he was dying. I don't think she really believed he *was* dying. Like it was all a trick to get me here."

"So why did you come? The money? I guess Dad owes you. You are his daughter."

"I came to see *you,*" Courtney said simply. "I wanted desperately to see you more than anything else in life. You're a woman and you're so *beautiful.*" Courtney's blue gaze was full of the old love and admiration.

"Pleeze!" Darcy was desperate not to display an ounce of softness. She didn't *know* her sister. She didn't *know* if the sweetness was real or assumed to make Courtney's short stay on Murraree easier.

"You're like Grandma." Courtney let her eyes move over her sister's face and the willow delicacy of her tall frame.

"The colouring, the set of your eyes and brows." She found she was trembling so much with emotion, she had to settle herself into an armchair. "Mum would do anything to make it up to you, Darcy. So would I."

"Well that's nice of you, but it's too late now, my dear." Darcy stuffed her hands into her jeans pockets in case she reached out to her sister. "The damage has been done, Courtney. To you and to me. We grew up apart. I loved you once but we can never get back to that. The results of separation have been too profound."

They went into their father's bedroom together, but Jock McIvor only had eyes for his younger daughter. Darcy might not have existed so blinkered was his vision.

I should have taken a bet on it, Darcy thought. I love him but people are right. He's one son of a gun. I've heard it for years but I did everything I could to block it out. Just how many times had she found McIvor lacking and forgiven him?

"Courtney!" Now McIvor was gesturing with his withered hand for her pretty as a picture sister to come close.

Last minute bonding, Darcy thought bleakly. McIvor was obviously desperate to get on the right side of God.

"Father," Courtney answered, her voice trembling. She was still afraid of him from the look in her eyes, even though McIvor seemed as though his heart could stop at any moment.

"He wants you to go to the bedside," Darcy prompted, dead set against showing protectiveness but protective all the same. It was as if they had moved back in time. The big sister with the little sister who had to be protected from her blustering father. "It's okay." She nodded reassuringly. "He's failing very fast."

"Come with me," Courtney begged.

Another pattern from the past.

"It's *you* he wants," Darcy murmured, absolutely beyond jealousy. Such were life's ironies she was fast learning.

"What are you two whispering about?" McIvor demanded

querulously, a frown gathering. "Always whispering. No need to stay, Darcy. I'm not going to eat her."

"I want Darcy to stay," Courtney spoke up. She crossed the Persian rug with its rich glowing colours to stand beside the bedside.

"Don't I get a kiss?" McIvor asked.

It was frightfully hypocritical. McIvor was giving a perfect imitation of the loving father with the prodigal child.

Does he really deserve a kiss? Darcy thought, standing well back so she could ponder life's mysteries. One thing was certain. This was Courtney's fifteen minutes of fame.

Courtney bent over him gracefully like a daffodil on a stalk, planting a quick kiss on McIvor's deeply scored forehead. "I'm sorry you're so desperately ill," she said, as pity consumed her. The wasted figure in the bed bore no resemblance to the man she remembered. *None!* That man had been a giant, splendidly fit and handsome, with brilliant blue eyes and a deep booming voice. This man's voice was a hoarse whisper. His lips were blue. There was even a blue tint to his grey skin. His hands on the coverlet trembled. He looked ready to expire.

"I'm dying, my girl," McIvor said poignantly, whether to make Courtney feel guilty or not Darcy didn't know. She was learning new things every day. Her father had never adopted that tone with her. Never got his tongue around it. "I wanted to see you before I breathed my last," McIvor told Courtney staring into her lovely face like she was an angel who had come to escort him to Heaven. "You're even more beautiful than your mother."

Courtney gently shook her head, staring down at her father in surprise. The intervening years had changed him. He was so different to how he had been then. So totally different to what she had expected.

"I keep that portrait in my room to remind me." McIvor gestured towards the opposite wall.

Courtney turned to follow his gaze. Her vision had been

so trained on the man in the bed she had failed to notice anything else. "How extraordinary!" she whispered. She began to wonder if there was a possibility she had judged her father too harshly. "You must have cared about her?"

"Of course I cared about her," McIvor claimed, as though his love had never burned out.

He's not having any difficulty lying Darcy thought. Probably his whole life had been littered with lies.

"And you," McIvor added, grasping Courtney's hand. "I blame all our unhappiness on your mother, child. She behaved very badly. She broke the sacred marriage bond."

Clearly that's the way he saw it, Darcy thought, wanting to quit the room and bang the door. And what did you do, Dad? Hit on every attractive woman in sight? Darcy felt like she was awakening from a distorted dream. Apparently her father's marriage vows had adultery written into them. It was starting to seem like she'd been brain washed as Curt had long claimed.

"Mum missed Darcy terribly," Courtney was saying. "I did too. We were so unhappy."

McIvor gave a terrible smile, lips drawn back from his teeth like a tiger. "She managed to cope though, didn't she? She soon found herself another man. You mother may have abandoned me but still, my girl, we share a powerful bond. You *are* my daughter and I want to leave you well provided for."

"I have a good job I enjoy." Courtney answered swiftly as though trying to head him off.

"What does this job involve?" The fatherly pose slipped again. The question came out like a sneer, in keeping with his long held view Courtney would turn out like her mother to be a bit of fluff.

"I'm personal assistant to the top woman in a public relations firm. The competition for my job was intense."

"So you're clever like your sister?" McIvor cut a bitterly

sarcastic grunt short. "You'll be able to open your own firm with what I'll be leaving you. More than you could possibly make in a dozen lifetimes. You two girls—" only now did his gaze shift to Darcy who was reduced to supporting herself against a gigantic rosewood cabinet-on-chest "—will be heiresses. The McIvor heiresses. Is there some man you're mixed up with?" He shot Courtney a piercing stare she didn't appear uncomfortable with.

"I have lots of male friends," she said calmly.

"You would! The men would be swarming around you like bees around the honey pot," he harrumphed.

It would be fair to say they did but Courtney answered modestly. "There's no-one special in my life at the moment."

"I'm glad to hear it," McIvor said. Affairs were all right for him. That didn't include his daughters. "After I'm gone, the two of you will become a mark for all sorts of unscrupulous characters and it will happen quickly. You must be protected. I've made arrangements for that. Your sister will tell you all about it." He patted Courtney's hand in a way that suggested he'd been deprived of her for far too long. "You're going to stay with me, aren't you?"

Darcy watched in amazement. Her father appeared to be speaking with genuine intensity. She had an impulse to cry out: " I'm over here, Dad. I'm Darcy, remember? The one who stayed." Her father's reactions were so strange. He was acting positively *loving* towards Courtney, as if he desperately needed to make up for her loss, when he had never spoken of his younger daughter. Not for many years and then as though her loss didn't matter. Perhaps Jock McIvor had a deadly fear of meeting his Maker. Darcy was seeing a side of her father she had never seen before.

"That was awful," Courtney gasped, when they were out in the long hallway jam-packed with enough consoles and mahogany chairs to fill an antique shop. "I didn't know my own father. He's changed beyond all recognition."

"That's what a couple of heart attacks and a stroke do to you," Darcy said. "Only six months ago he still looked marvellous." Darcy kept her tone dispassionate when she was feeling profoundly upset. "His first heart attack shook him to the foundations. He thought he was indestructible. When it came it came all at once."

"And you weren't going to tell us?"

"You're kidding!" Darcy's tone was bleak. "I didn't identify with you any more, Courtney. It's as simple as that."

"Please tell me you don't resent my coming here now, Darcy?" Courtney spoke haltingly as though it pained her.

"I'm struggling not to, but it's quite a task. I'm only human."

"I don't want the money. I don't need to be an heiress."

"Crazy as *that* sounds." Darcy scoffed. "Who knocks back money?"

"Whatever there is belongs to *you,*" Courtney said, desperate to get closer to the sister she had missed for so long. She had lots of girlfriends but no one could take Darcy's place. "You were the one who stayed. Adam told me you've been an enormous asset to Father; that you do a marvellous job on Murraree. You always did love the land."

"I would hope now you're a woman you will too," Darcy surprised herself by saying. "Dad didn't handle you right. He was such a bully. He's said in the past he had no talent for being a husband. There's a good chance he had no talent for being a father either."

They found Curt and Adam talking companionably in the old plant filled conservatory at the rear of the homestead. The external steel framed glass walls were almost enveloped in an extravagantly flowering cerise bouganvillea that turned the very air rosy. Both men stood up as the two sisters moved into the room side by side, as complete a contrast in types as one could ever see.

Darcy looked like a high strung thoroughbred with the upward tilt of her head, long neck, thick glossy mane and delicate racehorse legs, Curt thought. Golden haired Courtney was much shorter but she too held herself beautifully, the prettiness of her childhood firmed into adult loveliness. Although they couldn't have looked less alike both shared an air of intelligence, breeding and a quiet self-confidence for all the traumas associated with their childhood.

Darcy for her part watched in endless amazement as Curt and Courtney moved towards each other as if drawn by powerful magnets. It hit her right between the eyes. Curt and her radiant little sister? Well it didn't have *her* blessing. He bent his shapely head and kissed Courtney's apple blossom cheek. He hugged her. He *did* hug her. Even imperturbable Adam was looking hard in their direction as though he hadn't foreseen such an ardent welcome either. Adam's expression hardly evoked approval

And what of hers ? Did it mirror Adam's? It would have to be revealing. Not that anyone appeared to notice *her.* Courtney went very sweetly into Curt's arms, not even reaching his heart. Darcy's own heart gave a great sick lurch. Some trembling voice inside her began to shriek. *Don't take him. He's mine. He's mine. He's always been mine.*

Curt didn't appear to know about it. Neither did Courtney. They were smiling at each other with open affection. Something more. Strong attraction? Darcy felt herself flush a hot red. It was all her own fault. She had blundered through her love life. Maybe Courtney was in search of a husband? No woman in her right mind could overlook Curt. But Curt was *her* rock and Darcy was ashamed she kept quiet about it. She really had become her own worst enemy. The sight of Curt and Courtney together filled her with something like dread. She needed time to assimilate it. She knew from the depths of her sick and sorry experience she couldn't bear seeing another woman in Curt's arms.

Even her own sister. Her own sister worst of all! Courtney would be much better at holding onto a man than she ever was. Courtney would know lots of things she didn't know. How to keep a man at her side. How to make him feel big and strong and cherished. Courtney clearly didn't have her pathetic hang-ups.

"Curt, how lovely to see you!" There was honey in Courtney's sweet voice. Emotional tears sparkled in her blue eyes as she looked wonderingly into Curt's striking face.

"Welcome back, Courtney," Curt responded in a way that would have made any woman's toes tingle. "How did the meeting with your father go?'

Ultimately Darcy pulled herself together. "Break out the trumpets. It was the return of the prodigal daughter." Her laugh was brittle. Surely it was extraordinary neither Courtney nor Curt had made any comment on the other's appearance. Curt might have been six-foot at sixteen when Courtney and her mother had left but he was just a boy. Now he was a marvellous looking man, intensely charismatic. Courtney for her part had been a child of ten. Now she was a vision of enchanting femininity. They surely couldn't have seen one-another in the meantime, could they? Darcy very nearly turned faint. Curt would have told her. *Wouldn't he?* She almost asked the question aloud but she felt undermined enough already. The answer could be really bad.

"I'll organise coffee," she said instead, covering her dismay and confusion with briskness. "Still black for you, Adam?"

"Yes, thank you." Adam responded almost solemnly. He was hard at it pondering the possibility Courtney was giving a performance for Curt's benefit. And what a performance. Little Ms Courtney McIvor had multiple talents.

"I'll help you," Courtney turned to offer, struck by the expression on her sister's high mettled face.

"No, thanks. You and my friend, Curt here, must have lots to catch up on." Darcy tried, but couldn't control the sarcasm. "Adam can explain all about the trust that Dad wanted set up and how it works."

"Trust?" Courtney looked worried. "Aren't you inheriting outright?"

"Your father had his reasons for wanting a trust to be set up, Courtney," Curt said, companionably drawing up a chair. "Adam and I are trustees. As Adam is the legal man I'll let him explain it to you thought it's simple enough. I'll give Darcy a hand in the kitchen. I'm hoping she'll find herself a housekeeper. I know a few suitable women who'd jump at the job."

"I can manage. I *have* managed," Darcy pointed out stiffly. "Really I'd hate another woman in the house."

"Having a housekeeper will give you more time to yourself," Curt said in a reasonable voice. "Besides the homestead is too large for one woman to get around."

"So is that a criticism?" Darcy demanded to know as they were walking away. "Have you been busy checking for dust?"

"What's eating you?" he asked, noting the high colour in her cheeks.

"I've learned one thing today," she informed him. "Nothing is *ever* as it seems."

In the privacy of the kitchen she asked the burning question. "You didn't seem much surprised by Courtney's appearance nor she by yours. If I didn't know differently I'd swear you two have met up sometime. Maybe when you're in Brisbane on business. Have you?" she asked fiercely, feeling the hammering of her heart.

Curt's chiselled mouth turned down. "How I've dreaded this day! I am *so* sorry, Darcy. I can't put a foot right with you. I should have known you wouldn't miss a trick. We didn't think it would do the slightest good to tell you. In fact a lot of harm."

"We, who's *we?*" Darcy was on the verge of hitting him.

"Mum and me," Curt said, taking a step nearer, not away. "You must remember our mothers were friends?"

"So? I thought *we* were friends? What are you talking about? Please tell me in under ten seconds because I'm going to explode!"

"You're worse than a fire cracker," he said as though the thought had suddenly struck him. "My mother was worried about them. She kept in touch."

"Kath did?" Darcy took it so badly she almost bent double. Katherine Berenger was the finest woman she knew. Darcy respected her immensely. That Kath of all people had never said a word!

"She didn't dare start anything lest it rebound on you. Your father would have reacted badly to any interference in his affairs. Your mother believed it was far too risky to anger him. She made my mother promise to keep their meetings a secret."

With one dismissive gesture, Darcy waved his explanation away. "I don't think I can handle this," she announced, looking as appalled as she felt. "Your mother helped me through the worst times yet she never confided in me?"

"Think about it, Darcy," he urged, his handsome face taut with strain. "If you were told you would have confronted your father. No question about it. You *know* what his reaction would have been. He'd have gone *ballistic*. You were no match for McIvor. He used to make strong men quail. My mother tried to offer you all the balm she could affirming your mother's love for you. The terrible position she was in."

"Her *love* for me!" Darcy's laugh was wild. "It wasn't enough to make her stay. Some women stay with their children no matter what. Abusive husbands, poverty, isolation. She wouldn't stay, much less risk taking me."

"She was so desperately unhappy she couldn't remain with your father. She couldn't continue sleeping with the enemy."

Darcy stared at him. "I'll never forgive you." Her words rang loudly in the silent kitchen.

"That's not the worst thing you've done to me," he responded harshly.

"I feel like *everyone* has deserted me. I trusted you, Curt, as much as it's possible to trust anybody. I revered your mother. And you've both lied to me."

"Not lied, Darcy. We simply couldn't tell you without betraying your mother and upsetting you dreadfully. There was no way your father was going to let you go. You were the one he'd decided to keep. It was bad enough for you without causing more trauma. You would *not* have been allowed to go to your mother. Your father has lived his life as a powerful and in his way dangerous man. A very physical man given to unpredictable courses of action. He did threaten your mother and she took those threats seriously as well she might."

Elaborately Darcy turned her slender back to him, her deeply entrenched feelings of betrayal coming to the fore. She began to make the coffee setting out cups and saucers as if on autopilot. She'd actually gone to the trouble of making a fruit cake now she sliced through it as vigorously as if she were chopping through a timber log. "Damn you, Curt," she said tightly.

"Oh...Darcy," he said in exasperation. "Don't make yourself suffer any more." He was driven to catch her by the shoulders feeling the delicate bones beneath his hands. "Do you think I didn't *want* to tell you? Do you think I wanted to carry the burden?"

"Why the hell not?" she cried explosively. "You tell me everything else!" Darcy felt the angry tears spring to her eyes. "You criticise me at every turn. You criticise my father. You've questioned every aspect of our relationship. You've made me so mad! Why I damned nearly let you mess up my life. I enslaved my pride."

She saw the mirror of her anger in his brilliant green eyes.

"That's good coming from you!" The hands that had been so gentle turned to steel. "I can't imagine your life more messed up than it already *is*."

For a moment Darcy stared back at him in sheer hate. Driven to frenzy she raised her hand, cracking it across his handsome, determined, arrogant face.

That got a bitter derisive laugh. "At least I got some passion from you," he taunted with angry triumph.

She experienced a great pang of conscience and self-disgust. "I'm sorry." Her heart was banging against her rib cage so hard it might have been trying to get out. "I'm not myself. Let me go." She tried to pull away but he held on, shaking his head.

"Why?" Curt too was fighting for composure. "Why can't you look at me? Is it because when I touch you, you can't pretend any more?"

The truth, the truth and nothing but the truth! She was vibrating all over when she well knew the dangers of provoking Curt. It played havoc with her. "Take pity on me!" It came out like a lament.

"You don't deserve pity. You deserve a good shake up."

"I *am* shaken up!" A helpless desire reached out its tendrils for her. "My whole world has been turned upside down. I hate to be deceived." By Curt of all people.

"No one could be better at deceiving herself than you." Curt threw up his hands, his contempt barely veiled. "Maybe you'll feel differently about things when you calm down."

She took great care to move out of his orbit though Mars wouldn't be far enough. "My *sister* too has kept me in the dark. Another thing I have to grapple with. She could have told me right at the start she'd met up with you and your mother over the years."

"Like me she'd been instructed not to," Curt argued their case. "Hell, it couldn't have been more than a dozen times. I wasn't part of the meetings. Certainly not for years. Of recent times I've been the one collecting my mother to take her back to our hotel after their rendezvous. It was a courtesy to say a few words at the same time."

"Yet a friendship developed, damn it! Courtney went into your arms like she belonged there."

Curt shook his head in disbelief. "You can't be jealous?"

There was nothing she could say to that but admit it. "You have to *love* someone to be jealous," she told him, still wearing her scars. "There's no point in taking this any further. I'm bitterly disappointed in you."

"It would be a miracle if you weren't!" His face grim Curt took charge of the trolley. "You're not going to take it out on Courtney, are you?"

Darcy tried desperately to gather herself in when she really felt like letting out a great cry of anguish. Courtney's blue eyes had smitten their father. Now it seemed Curt had fallen under their spell. "You make it sound like I'm a real bitch."

"To be honest, sometimes you are. It's about the only time you get in touch with your feminine side. Courtney on the other hand is a very sweet girl. You can't look at her without smiling."

That fairly summed up Courtney. Child and woman. Dread was like ice water in Darcy's veins and under that a blind fear. "Don't men love sweet little things," she said mournfully, trying not to crumble.

"Can you blame us?" Curt mocked. "Most men go in search of peace."

"And I hate men!" Blue lightning flashed from her black fringed eyes. "A little while ago that hell raiser, Jock McIvor, was playing the part of the loving father to the hilt. Unlike the bad old days he and my little sister got on just fine. In fact all it would take is a little planning and a little help for Courtney to scoop the pool. A fortune awaits her. I daresay Dad who has re-invented himself as the long suffering father will want *her* to sit by his bedside."

"Maybe atonement has gone to his head," Curt suggested acidly. "It's not such a bad idea anyway. *You* might be able to get some sleep at night. You sure need it. You're nearly jumping out of your skin."

CHAPTER FOUR

IT SEEMED entire Outback Queensland came to the funeral. Trucks, buses, four-wheel drives private and charter planes. And that was without counting the inter-state mourners who knew better than to ignore Big Jock McIvor even in death. They all toiled in procession in the blazing sun to the McIvor family cemetery, a distance from Murraree's homestead. Several of the mourners, big serious-faced, superbly fit cattle men, Curt one of them, carried the ornate casket with what appeared to be surprising ease. The casket was fit for a king. Beautifully grained polished wood, bronze handles, a gleaming brass plaque. The deceased had insisted upon it being carried, though it could just as easily have come on the back of one of the station's utes Darcy thought keeping her half hooded eyes trained on the ground.

I am not going to break down. Not now.

She had expected tender-hearted Courtney who in their father's last days had established herself as Jack McIvor's favourite to be weeping copiously—she must know every eye was on her—but Courtney did not. She stood at her elder sister's shoulder, dry eyed.

Not a hypocrite anyway.

They were both dressed head to foot in black. Another final edict from Jock. Black dresses, wide brimmed black hats, black pumps. The sombreness of the outfit was unbelievably becoming to Courtney with her halo of shining blonde hair and big cornflower blue eyes. Darcy thought she looked more like a crow, several of which were circling overhead. Adam Maynard stood next to Courtney, tall and elegant, making her look touchingly small.

Impossible to believe you're dead, Dad.

But he *was* dead. Darcy had stood at his bedside, hearing him breathe his last. Her tears had been on full view then. They had rolled unchecked down her face so that Curt's mother, Kath, who had flown over to Murraree with her son to be with the sisters, Darcy in particular, had passed her a handkerchief and Courtney who felt herself unaccepted had grasped her sister's hand, trying to give as much love and support as she could.

Finally they were all gathered around the open grave while the pall bearers lowered the casket with slings into the ground. Now the robed minister, a handsome man with a large steel grey head and the pious expression of someone in daily communication with God, began to speak. Unbelievably ponderously. To Darcy's ears it sounded like an unnatural voice. An actor playing an eccentric vicar perhaps, but Jock had wanted this particular churchman, celebrated for his eulogies, to conduct the service. The minister lived up to his reputation, giving weighty significance to Jock McIvor's extraordinary and blameless life. It was a view that could only be brought out for special occasions when one only speaks good of the dead.

Dad is at last respectable.

Someone, Darcy didn't look up to see who it was, had a coughing fit. Maybe there was only a certain amount the mourners were prepared to accept without registering a veiled protest. Darcy was glad of the shade of a huge desert oak. It was one of many that encircled the graveyard that was enclosed by a black wrought iron fence so tall it could have kept out a team of camels. This quiet place looking out over the rolling red sand hills held the remains of generations of

McIvors including in one small section guarded by a beautiful white marble angel, the children who had not survived their infancy in the far off days when the Outback was without the mantle of safety of The Flying Doctor.

When the time came McIvor's older daughter Darcy emptied a small scoop of red ochre earth on top of the gleaming casket, handing the brass scoop to a pallbearer and stepping quietly back.

Whatever you were, Dad, I loved you. Go in peace.

Just when she thought she couldn't take anymore without fainting—she'd been unable to eat properly for days—it was over.

At least it was over until they all toiled back to the house.

"Darcy?" Katherine Berenger's voice was solicitous, tender with affection. "You're *very* pale, dear. You can't walk back to the house." Katherine looked about for her son, who was standing several feet away at the centre of a group of men.

"Neither can I in these shoes." Courtney, who was also pale and shaken, pulled a little face. "Was that, I wonder, our father, the minister was talking about?"

"I expect Dad wrote the whole thing and the minister delivered it," Darcy answered.

Kath had caught her son's attention. Now Curt strode towards them. Crystal clear green eyes glittered in his tanned face. He too wore black with a black tie and a shirt white as snow. He had to be feeling the full weight of his jacket in the heat, but he gave no sign of it. As usual he looked dynamic, not subject to heat, rain or cold like mere mortals.

"You're not going to walk back." He spoke to Darcy directly, scrutinizing her pale, stressed out face carefully. He laid one hand on his mother's shoulder. "I've organised for vehicles to take the women back to the homestead."

"Of course you have, darling," Kath nodded thankfully. Her son had a habit of never forgetting anything.

"This is a day that will change all our lives," Darcy announced to them all in a far-away voice, then in the next instant pitched sideways into Curt's waiting arms.

Everyone had moved away from the silent graveyard. Even the birds had left.

"You don't really have to attend at the house," Curt said. They were sitting on a stone bench in the shade waiting for Darcy to fully recover.

"Of course I do!" She fanned herself with her wide brimmed hat. "What do you think Dad would have said if I didn't make it? On the other hand, would he even have noticed? It's not exactly what I expected and certainly Courtney didn't invite it, but Dad in this last week behaved as though he didn't know who the hell I was."

Curt took her hand in his and shook her fingers. "Jock's *gone.* He lived his life like a drama. He was forever playing a part, going for the Academy Award."

Darcy frowned. "Wouldn't you try to be as true to yourself as you could when you were hurtling into eternity? It was all I could do to get near him. It *had* to be Courtney. Doesn't that strike you as weird?"

"Just about everything your father did struck me as weird," Curt freely admitted. "Don't take it to heart. He hadn't seen Courtney since she was a child. He hadn't forgotten about her for all he said. She's so like her mother. Don't let it upset you, Darcy."

"Well it does. It makes me feel as though *no one* wanted me. My mother and at the end, my father. The question is, *why?* Am I so unloveable?" She began fanning herself again, forcing coolness onto her face.

Curt took the hat from her, waving it less frantically but more effectively. "Given Jock reared you the wonder is you're as loveable as you are."

"What?" She turned to stare at him, catching the half smile on his mouth. "Gee thanks."

"You're looking better," he noted with relief her colour was returning.

"Good thing I have you to fall back on. Literally."

"You're a featherweight, Darcy. You're burning yourself out."

"And you want to change that?" She rose slowly to her feet, testing herself, slender as a lily in her well cut black linen shift.

"That's what I wanna do," he mocked, twirling her hat in his hand. "You don't want this, do you?" He too stood up, nicely towering over her. He had taken off his jacket, loosened his tie. A lock of mahogany hair fell onto his smooth tanned forehead.

He looked like a movie star who just happened to be a cattle man. "Not until the next funeral," she said mordantly.

"Really it should stay with Jock."

To her shocked surprise he used the hat like a Frisbee. She watched it land unerringly in the open grave that station hands would shortly fill in.

"Hell," Darcy breathed in amazement. "Now I won't have any hat to wear."

"I'll buy you another one." His voice was as smooth as satin. "One that suits you."

Colour smudged her cheeks. "It was the best I could do at short notice."

"Only kidding!" He glanced down on her. "I've never seen you look so exotic. I suppose we'd better make it back to the house. Say goodbye to Jock unless you plan on visiting him every day."

Darcy shook her head. "I loved him," she said. "Muggins is my name. I thought he loved me. I thought I was his only true confidante, not that he consulted me before he made any important decision. Let's face it. Love was unobtainable from Jock. He was one of those steely hard men who can function without it."

Despite the fact she spoke with no trace of self-pity the poignancy of her words pierced Curt's heart.

At the homestead Katherine Berenger, a statuesque woman with hair like dark burnt honey, much admired and respected in the far flung community, held the fort effortlessly as was her way. A stream of people were making their way up to Courtney, kindly in their manner, sincere with their sympathies, but unmistakably agog with curiosity at how she'd turned out. The whole Outback knew the story of Jock McIvor's failed marriage. How the young sisters had been split between both parents with the inevitable traumas. Little Courtney had turned out very well indeed was the general opinion. She was as lovely as her mother, whom many people remembered, and her manner was charming if understandably subdued.

In a rare moment when she was briefly on her own, Adam Maynard found his way to her side, not so much to engage her in conversation but continue his study of her. "For a wake everyone appears to be eating and drinking with abandon," he murmured near her ear. "How are you bearing up?"

She tilted her blonde head to look at him, meeting brilliant dark eyes she found strangely unfathomable. "It's Darcy I'm worried about."

"Curt will look after her," he said soothingly. "They should be here soon."

"I don't know where she finds the strength," Courtney said, still in a worried tone. "She's hardly slept and it's been difficult to get her to eat. Father meant so much to her."

Adam inclined his head. "He was all she had. It's a very lonely isolated existence out here. It must have been extremely difficult for Darcy growing up without a mother. A mother's influence and gentle ways. You at least had that."

Oversensitive to the issue Courtney thought she detected

an edge in his suave tones. "I had to learn how to survive, too, Adam. Neither Darcy nor I had a choice. It was our parents who separated us."

"Could neither of you—your mother and you—ever find the time to contact her?" he asked, looking down into that exquisite, flower-like face that could be hiding so much.

"What are you waiting for, Adam?" Courtney wasn't a McIvor for nothing. She fired up. "For me to say how guilty I feel?" Although he had been courtesy itself to her during his stay-over at Murraree Courtney had the sinking feeling Adam Maynad was highly suspicious of her. A state of affairs that made her uneasy. "I *do* feel guilty. More than you realize apparently. You don't like me, do you?"

His dark eyes held hers keenly. The sombreness of her silk dress only accentuated the enchanting blue and gold of her colouring and the apple blossom skin. "Why would you say that? If I've offended you, I'm sorry."

She shook her head dismissively. "You don't expect me to believe that, do you, Adam? Everything you say has planning behind it."

"You don't find lawyers attractive as a species?" He smiled at her.

"How can you expect me to find you attractive when all along I've had the feeling you've been silently judging me."

"I hope you're not going to pretend you haven't been sizing me up as well?" he countered with a lift of one eyebrow. "I have noticed the sharp intelligence in those flower blue eyes."

The normally sweet natured Courtney bristled. Arresting as he was, she didn't have the friendly rapport with him as she had with Curt, for instance. Beneath the civility a strange antagonism ran like an electric current. "Don't put too much store on it. The fact Father seemed to need me around in his last days wasn't something I invited."

"I'm sure I've never suggested any such thing," he answered suavely. "Where did you get *that* idea?"

"Maybe it's the way you look down your arrogant nose at me," she said. "If you're looking for an angle, you won't find one. I am not an opportunist. Father wanted me here. It's on record in your letter."

"He was such an unpredictable man," Adam murmured.

"You don't have to tell *me* that. We must suppose he felt guilty about me."

"He had reason to," Adam said dispassionately.

"And I don't want his money," Courtney continued in a low, tight voice that was not characteristic of her. "Money had nothing to do with why I came here."

He bowed slightly. "I stand chastised."

"I was longing to see my sister," she said. "I idolized Darcy when I was a child."

"She's a remarkable young woman," Adam agreed quietly, staring over Courtney's head. "She and Curt have just entered the house," he informed her, his eyes returning to Courtney's expressive face.

"Then you'll excuse me, Adam." Courtney's voice and manner couldn't have been cooler. She turned on her high heels and walked away.

Adam looked after her, her chin in the air, all graceful scorn. She had the serene beauty of an angel but was she as innocent as she seemed? Adam couldn't get the question out of his mind. Particularly when at the last moment Jock McIvor had required changes to his will.

It was midmorning of the next day and they were all assembled in Jock McIvor's study. It was so crowded with objects and artifacts it would have been difficult for a visitor to know where to look first. Adam was seated behind McIvor's mammoth desk which would have accommodated a parliamentary front bench, in McIvor's custom made black leather swivel chair. McIvor had never been comfortable with anything that wasn't *big.* Curt, by his own decision, sat to Adam's right, the two sisters had comfortable arm chairs drawn up for them in front of the desk. Courtney, seated, was looking anxious, Darcy was standing, rocking back on her high heeled boots, full of fight. A portrait of their deceased father, marvellously flamboyant, hung on the wall behind the desk, dominating the room. It was McIvor in his prime, his vast sexual appeal apparent. Forty-five years of age; a big handsome aggressive man with a dent in his chin, a fiery leonine mane and calculating sapphire blue eyes, a colour that was repeated in the casual open necked shirt he wore with his work denims. A rakish touch was a scarlet bandanna he wore loosely tied around his neck.

Bookcases and cabinets that held all his sporting trophies completely covered another two walls along with an extensive collection of framed photographs of Jock with Prime Ministers, parliamentarians, pastoralists, relatives, various visiting V.I.P.'s, in one, his arm flung around the slim shoulders of a visiting screen star of yesteryear. The far wall was hung with all kinds of aboriginal artefacts some of them pretty gruesome. McIvor had grown up in a world where the kurdaitcha man in his special slippers made from emu feathers stuck together with blood carried out many a revenge expedition.

"Let's get cracking," Curt said, his handsome features businesslike. "Darcy, could I prevail on you to sit down?"

"I still have some thinking to do." Darcy's eyes were jewel bright. "To think Dad couldn't trust us with our own money!" She tossed her head. Her sable mane for once was not confined in a plait but tied at the nape with a silk scarf.

"The short answer to that is *no*. There's no use getting hostile with us. We're just trying to do a job thrust upon us," Curt explained.

"What a joy that must be!"

"Your father didn't move with the times, Darcy," he said patiently. "He followed his own rules. To be fair he genuinely believed there would be problems in allowing you to take control of the estate."

"What about you, Curt?" she challenged. "You believed it as much as Dad did. All men are despots. They want control. They don't want to hand over any power to women. Until they do we'll *never* be free."

"Hear, hear!" Courtney suddenly exploded. "I for one am quite capable of looking after myself. I *know* Darcy is."

"Capable of looking after yourselves in the normal sense," Adam intervened. "It can't be forgotten your late father was a multi-millionaire with a big portfolio. Handling it would cause a lot of business men trepidation. You haven't been singled out solely because you're women."

"Please, Adam, don't insult our intelligence," Darcy scoffed. "You know darn well that's exactly the case. Curt didn't even begin to deny it."

Curt looked up at her, feeling like throwing up his own hands in despair. "I doubt at this point you even know how much your father was worth, Darcy? He let you in on his affairs up to a point. After that, you were kept very much in the dark. That's the way he wanted it."

"In retrospect I should have stood on my own two feet," Darcy fumed. "Instead of doing everything I could to support him, I should have made a life for myself. Isn't that what you've always told me, Curt?"

"Did you *ever* listen?" he fired back. "What's done is done, Darcy. The caravan moves on and we have to move with it. Try and look on it as though you're getting a good team to support you."

"Oh thank you, Curt," Darcy said with extreme sarcasm, hauling back her chair and sitting down. "That means you and

Adam and the other lawyer who didn't have the decency to get here—"

"He's overseas, Darcy. We told you that."

Darcy ignored Curt and his testy expression. "Are going to be our Protectors?" She turned to look at her sister. "Is that clear to you, Courtney? Curt and Adam here are going to be our Protectors. We have to go to them cap in hand to ask for everything we want. Curt, I believe, has power of attorney."

"Darcy, it's not going to be a serious problem unless you're hell bent on making it one," he said. "I repeat, I prefer you to look on us as a team. Your father felt he could trust me. Strange after all these years you've decided you don't."

"Things have changed," Darcy said darkly. "It all comes down to power. I thought I was being trained to take over but all along my father was opposed to that. He believed women didn't understand the first thing about power. I supported him in every way I could. I gave him all the encouragement in the world and what did he do? He rewarded me by handing over my inheritance to *you!*"

"You've forgotten Courtney," Curt pointed out with as much patience as he could, giving Courtney a sympathetic glance.

"Don't worry about me, Curt," Courtney said gently. "I've been standing on my own two feet for quite a while." Having said that she flashed Adam a quelling glance as though he had spoken out against her. "I don't want even a slice of our father's estate."

"What *do* you want?" Darcy flashed, "the whole pie?" She felt shame at saying it, but all morning she'd been intercepting some quite unendurable melting glances between her sister and Curt. She had to acknowledge beneath her anger was an unacknowledged emotion. Sexual jealousy. It made her want to scream.

Courtney's lovely skin coloured up. She looked bitterly rejected. "That's not fair."

"Fair?" Darcy's over wrought voice cracked. "From the moment you arrived, you fulfilled all Dad's expectations a thousand times over. I got pretty short shrift in his last days. Anyway, what the hell!" Darcy threw up her hands in self-disgust.

Curt recognised her sense of betrayal. "For once I agree with you, Darcy. Now, may we now get on with the discussion?"

"I just want you to know, Curt, I have enormous respect for you," Darcy looked at him directly, challengingly. "You too, Adam. McIvor's daughters need top financial brains to handle their affairs seeing they lack a brain between them."

"We understand how you feel, Darcy," Adam said, and he did. "You've worked so hard, you've sacrificed so much, you've lost your father, I know your heartache."

"What do you know about *me?*" Courtney demanded of him, her voice stripped of its normal sweetness. "I find it very strange you're remarkably unsympathetic to me."

"Darcy was the one who stayed with her father," Adam argued mildly, but there was a confrontational note in his voice as well.

"I should tell you now," Curt intervened, giving Darcy a serious glance, "in his last days your father made several changes to his will."

"No, what else is new?" Darcy pleaded.

"You're having us on, aren't you?" Courtney asked warily.

"I'm deadly serious, Courtney," Curt responded, looking across the huge desk.

"Well he installed Courtney as his favourite," Darcy continued to address Curt. "Once she arrived he didn't want a bar of me. Courtney is Dad's heiress? Go on, surprise us." Curt wouldn't be averse to a rich bride. A beautiful one to boot.

"It appears your father developed a great deal of feeling for Courtney in those last days." Adam's clever, hawkish face was impassive.

"It had nothing to do with me!" Courtney protested,

thinking her worst fears were being confirmed. "Dying people often get contrary. If he appeared to have forgotten Darcy—"

Darcy leapt to her feet, her heart beating a frenzied drum. "What do you mean, appeared? He *did!*"

"Your father wanted you to share *equally,*" Curt said, endorsing what Adam had said. "That doesn't mean I don't think you shouldn't fight it, Darcy. Adam and I don't believe you'd have a problem. It's patently unfair."

"I agree!" Courtney tried to reach out for her sister, but Darcy was on a roll. She flashed her startling, aquamarine eyes. "I'm not listening to any more of this. I have difficulty believing what I'm hearing. If my father were a *real* man, instead of a moral coward, he would have come right out and told me to my face. I had no problem with Courtney getting a share. A substantial share, but, excuse me, not the bloody *lot.*"

"It isn't the lot, Darcy," Adam said. "You could fight it in any case."

"With the money *you're* going to give me?" she retorted, wound up like a spring. "Wouldn't that be a conflict of interest seeing you're Courtney's trustees too."

Courtney stood up, taking a quick step towards her sister. "Forgive me, Darcy. I should never have come. The father who ignored me for nearly all my life took to me on a delirious whim. It wasn't *real.* It was designed to get him through the pearly gates. I was a passing source of wonder!"

"The golden haired, blue-eyed angel come down from Heaven," Darcy said it without anger but a tremendous amount of hurt. "You have the sweetest prettiest face, the prettiest profile just like when you were a little kid. The thing is, you *shone* in the darkness for him, Courtney. I didn't."

"Why don't we stop for a while," Curt suggested, rising swiftly to his feet.

"No keep going," Darcy urged, striding to the door. "For *me* it's ended! I'm only surprised Dad didn't turn me loose without a cracker."

"Oh dear, oh dear, oh dear, oh dear," Courtney moaned, her face betraying her extreme upset. "I never in my wildest dreams thought it was going to turn out this way."

Adam, hardening his heart, found he was critical of that. Women with faces like angels could influence all sorts of events.

"I'll go after her." There was dismay in Curt's smouldering eyes. "People didn't call Jock McIvor a ruthless bastard for nothing."

CHAPTER FIVE

HE HAD to break into an Olympic sprint to catch up with her. She was heading for the stables, already calling for Zack to saddle up Nabila, a proud and spirited ebony mare with a white star in the middle of her forehead. Nabila was an amalgam of thoroughbred and pure Arabian. It had been his present to Darcy on her twenty-first birthday, a present which had elicited from her tears of joy and in the dawn of the morning after, her virginity to which she had attached great importance.

It had been the most glorious, unforgettable idyll about which neither of them spoke as though it had happened in a dream.

Nabila was fast. Very fast. A princess among her own kind.

He could do nothing else but watch as Darcy took off on the mare's back, heading for the open plain. He knew what it felt like. Flying without wings.

In the mood she was in she could kill herself. Darcy was a lot more hot-blooded than she knew.

Zack, the part aboriginal stable boy, ran out to do Curt's bidding. "Ain't Miss Darcy somethin'?" he asked, his glossy amber face split in a smile. "I never seen her so mad. Goin' after her I expect? Centaur right for yah, Boss?" Zack figured Mr. Berenger would have no trouble with that one. Mr. Berenger was a horseman.

"Thanks, Zack and make it snappy. I don't want her to get too far ahead."

"She turn into a Spirit Woman right before me very eyes." Zack drew a wondering breath. "Miss Darcy can ride like the wind."

"When Allah created the horse he cried out to the South Wind: I will that a creature should proceed from thee," Curt found himself saying.

"No kiddin'?" Zack was impressed. "Gee, that's good, Boss. Who's this fella anyway?"

"Not fella, Allah. Forget it, Zack. I'm in a hurry."

Moments later Curt was galloping across the open plain on the silver-grey stallion Centaur which had been McIvor's favourite. The stallion responded to Curt's signals with lightning quickness, revelling in a good gallop when it had only been exercised and not ridden for some time. Though Zack and his pal Jaffa, another stable boy were as accomplished as many a successful jockey the stout hearted but temperamental Centaur was near to being a one-man horse.

Curt could see Darcy up ahead at full gallop, light as smoke on the mare's back. A good gallop wouldn't harm her so long as she stuck to the rolling open plains with its sea of wheat eared Mitchell grass. The top of the grass was embroidered with little gold centred gilla flowers so the stallion's flying hooves left a broad trail of crushed petals behind them.

Their mad gallop had excited the birds. Glorious coloured parrots, sulphur crested white cockatoos, pink and pearl galahs, the undulating legions of budgerigar. They filled the sky. Even a wedge tailed eagle, bigger and more powerful than the golden eagle of Europe stayed with him as though overseeing happenings.

What a piece of work was McIvor, Curt inwardly raged. It was only natural Courtney get something but Darcy who had given her father all her support had been betrayed. He had thought he and McIvor had thrashed out early Darcy would be the major beneficiary, but at the last minute McIvor had changed his instructions.

Curt had no difficulty recalling the conversation. "I know you don't agree with it, Curt, but as my appointed executor and trustee you have to respect my wishes. Now that I have seen Courtney again I won't have it any other way. Her sweetness and warmth have stirred my poor old heart. Darcy has nothing to complain about. She'll be a rich woman."

"So what's Courtney's secret?" Adam had asked him later in confidence, not bothering to hide his own suspicions. "It's easy for a beautiful woman to get under a man's guard. This clearly isn't going the way it was meant to go. I think we'd have to be pretty naïve to believe Courtney didn't influence her father's emotions. As a lawyer, I've never met a single soul who wasn't interested in the money. Courtney might say she isn't interested, but she'd be less than human if she weren't. Chances are she's like everybody else."

Swiftly the powerful stallion gained on the mare. How many times had he actually seen Courtney over the years? Less than a dozen. He had been prepared to stand by her but what did he really know about her? Next to nothing beyond the fact she had a lovely face and a very engaging manner. There wasn't the slightest hint of avarice about her. He was convinced of it. But one thing couldn't be discounted. She had been brought up by a mother who must have hated McIvor. Surely a bit of that hatred came out in the daughter? Jock McIvor was a trouble maker until the end of his days.

They had almost reached the hill country before the race was over.

Curt exhaled sharply. "Stop, Darcy!" he thundered, his handsome face grim.

The budgerigars decided to respond, dipping and flashing only a scant twenty feet over their heads.

Darcy did not, *could* not reply but gradually she gathered the mare in.

In the distance the mirage was flowing like a silver river. "Let's get out of the sun," Curt said, aware his presence was inflaming her more than calming her.

"Why are you here?" she demanded to know, looking glorious in her anger.

"Are you going to order me to leave?"

"How can I do that?" she asked in a voice that shook. "Everything is under your control."

"Don't be stupid, Darcy. Please don't be stupid," he begged. He had turned Centaur's head away from the jagged line of hills towards a waterhole a short distance off. It was screened by flat topped acacias and some purple bush fruit with a pearlescent sheen. In the heat the pond's glitter had enormous appeal.

The mare had automatically fallen into step with the stallion, both animal coats darkened with sweat.

Beneath the leafy canopy Curt dismounted first, tying the stallion's reins to a low branch. Darcy seemed to sway in the saddle. He went to her, reaching up to lift her down. Even when she was standing she didn't pull away as he expected but almost laid her head against his chest.

"Are you all right?" He stared down at her in concern. She had lost so much weight recently she was positively breakable.

"Sure." She jerked back immediately, removing the cream akubra that had been angled down hard on her head and throwing it onto a bed of bottle-green curling ferns. Curt attending to the mare, watching distractedly as Darcy walked away from him across the creamy-yellow sand, dotted with grey boulders of varying size. When she reached the moon shaped pond, she bent and splashed her overheated face with water.

He crossed the sand to join her, letting the surprisingly cold water run over his face and into his mouth, half drenching his shirt. "In the old days you'd be pulling off your clothes to go for a swim," he said.

"A swim isn't what I have in mind."

"Oh? Do you want to kill me first?"

She didn't deign to answer but pulled off her silk scarf with an unselfconscious air and began to dab her face dry.

Curt kept perfectly still, his stomach muscles contracting violently. Her beautiful sable hair swirled free around her face and over her shoulders. The beauty she sought to down play was fully exposed. Her cascading hair so thick and lustrous was the perfect frame for her fine boned oval face. Its darkness emphasized the startling colour of her eyes and the gold of her skin. Her mouth was luscious, full and soft, coloured a fuchsia pink to match her cotton shirt. The thin damp fabric revealed the taut nipples of her small, high breasts. They were unconfined. It was incredibly erotic

"How beautiful you are!" he said in an involuntary rush.

She looked up at him, caught the storm of expression in his eyes. An answering heat was wrapping her body in a tight sensuous veil. "We can't *do* this," she warned, shaking her head.

"Strangely enough *I'm* going to." An *immense* frustration overcame him. It couldn't be borne. "You can rant and rave later."

Before she could say another word, he caught her to him with such fierce mastery she was overwhelmed. What he demanded she was compelled to give. It seemed the natural order of things. All the old magic swam into her veins like thick sweet honey. Curt was a sorcerer casting another one of his spells. She had given him her love and she had taken it back. But surely a man could be allowed one mistake?

The passion of the encounter went a long way toward emptying the deep well of misery that had held her prisoner. For long moments she allowed her body to melt into his. The sensation was so bitter, so beautiful, she convulsively shuddered. Memories flooded into her mind. Of being naked with Curt poised above her, his eyes taking in every fact of her nakedness, her woman's body. She saw the pearl grey of the sky in the pre-dawn, felt the scented breeze blowing in from the desert in that year covered with wildflowers. Such memories lived on…and on…and on. Love's legacy.

He opened her lips like they were petals with his tongue, exploring the interior so slowly so voluptuously her head swam and all sense of caution slowed. His touch wasn't gentle. It was wonderfully *hungry.* So hungry the weight of longing soon became unbearable. Such a *knowing* kiss. Her lover's kiss. A lover too powerful. Curt could make her do anything he asked.

As he had then.

He had impregnated her body.

Her secret.

With a little cry Darcy jerked back her head, but he covered her breast with the palm of his hand. "No, don't," he muttered, his tone filled with urgency. "Don't pull away, Darcy. Please."

"You won't *let* me." She twisted and turned in a white heat.

"Because you're *mine!*" His strong hand, that moved with such conviction slipped the pearly buttons of her blouse as practised as if he did it every day. Man-like he sought her naked flesh.

Darcy flinched, even though she was unbearabley moved. Whatever her mind chose to do her body did another. She felt it turn to *fire.* She heard him sigh with the pleasure her body was giving him as he teased and caressed the nipple of her exposed breast.

She made a last urgent effort to stay him calling his name, but she doubted he even heard her. She never could break his intense concentration on her.

She struggled. He pinned her, bending her back in a tortuous curve. "Did you really think the charade was going to go on forever? I'm going to make this last."

Sensation jack-knifed through her body as his mouth found her pink nipple, bunched like a berry. His lips drew on its sweetness, his teeth ever so gently nipping. There were knife like little stabs in her groin. She hadn't forgotten those. His hand was sliding inside her jeans, his long fingers pressing down on her flat stomach, concentrating on reaching the secret folds of her body.

Couldn't she allow herself this bliss? God knows she wanted it. Wanted it with a near manic desire. She had tried sex with a few others but her experiences with Curt had completely traumatized her. She could feel the dampness of desire on the crotch of her briefs. Frantically she tried to push back against the cascades of passion. They weren't safe. She remembered the time she had blindly assumed it was safe. Stupid, negligent, motherless girl. It was impossible to keep a clear head when her whole body was ablaze.

Turn back the clock. Do it. You remember the way it was. The abandonment that always left you in tears of rapture and afterwards, despair.

Her body was screaming for release. *Do it!*

Of a sudden she felt sick. She should know better than anyone the price was too high. She'd been punished before. She'd be punished again.

"Curt...Curt!" She bucked against him. "Don't."

He shook his head like a maddened bull. "What's your problem, Darcy? Can't you for once admit this is what you *want?*"

She laughed wildly. "You know me. There's always a problem!" Her laugh almost turned into a howl. She threw out supplicating hands.

For long moments he stared at her in all her staggering beauty. Intent on his own driving passion, pity began to trickle through the great wall of desire. His voice had a jagged edge, but understanding too. "Life has done a job on you, Darcy girl," he said almost sorrowfully. "Come here to me." He gathered her back in, cradling her like a child in his arms. "What is it about women who treat men badly? We keep coming back for more. You need help, Darcy. Just tell me this. Are you swearing off sex for the rest of your life?"

She moaned, the weight of her history heavy on her heart. "Sex is the most dangerous thing in the world. It can be truly wonderous but it can ruin lives."

He gave her a long uncomprehending look but she averted her face. He wanted her so much he wasn't entirely certain what he was going to do next. This woman drove him crazy. "Maybe you're saving yourself for the right man?" he suggested with black humour. "Frankly if I were you I wouldn't wait all that much longer. Even I have to get married some time. My mother demands it. She feels deprived without grandchildren. Sunset needs an heir. Only a complete fool, dedicated to masochism, would wait for you."

"I'll kill you if you get married!" she said tightly.

He gazed down on her for long moments. "You're quite simply…mad."

"I am." She broke away, making such a mess of doing up her buttons, Curt with a muffled oath did it for her.

"But you won't let *me* save you. Well, it's only fair to tell you I'm thinking about marriage very seriously. I've never got any promises out of you."

He couldn't know the great surge of pain she felt. "You could have any woman you liked." Her own sister with the blue eyes and the golden curls?

"That's right," he confirmed grimly. "Which is why you should pay attention. Come to think of it my brain must be scrambled trying to get any normal reaction out of you. We'd better go back to the house. I'm about a hair's breadth away from putting you through a fate worse than death."

"I'm sorry, so sorry." She moaned afresh.

"About *what* precisely?" He took a handful of her hair and

tipped her face to him. "Darcy, you're a mystery to me. I loved you. I loved you. I could literally have loved you to the death but you didn't think my love was worth it. You've done everything in your power to kill it."

"At least I can't say I'll die unloved." Her little laugh cracked.

"What went wrong between us, Darcy?" he asked, his eyes deadly serious.

She flinched a little. "I promise I'll tell you one day."

"Tell me now."

She wasn't capable of doing it. "No," she said in a tight voice. "It's not good."

"Of course it's not bloody good." Even his rage was weary. "It's sick. You let your father ruin your life. You let that old bastard turn you off me. Who knows what he said. He was a man who had no scruples about achieving his own ends. I thought *you* loved me. You certainly acted like it. But it wasn't so. Aah...let's forget it," he released her in total self-disgust. "Pretend none of it happened. It's all water under the bridge anyway." He turned away from her, speaking over his shoulder. "Before we ride back, I have to advise you as your friend at least to stop flailing yourself about the will. Fight it or accept it. The hard unpalatable fact is your father had a right to do whatever he wanted with his money."

"Of course he did," she cried. "I'm amazed he included me at all. First thing tomorrow I'm going to send away for a big stamp that says: Rejected."

"Well get one for me." He headed away from her, his lean powerful body taut.

Darcy found herself running after him. "You and Courtney have become very pally." She stared up at his carved profile. "Do you suppose my little sister who appears so angelic drove a wedge between Dad and me? Could she possibly do that?"

Curt stopped in his tracks. "Darcy, I would truly hate to think so," he said.

"You couldn't hate it more than me," Darcy answered sadly. "Those blue eyes of hers would melt any man's heart."

The same thought had crossed Adam Maynard's mind many times since he had first laid eyes on the lovely Ms. Courtney McIvor. Very likely she'd left a string of broken hearts in her wake he considered, with the cynicism she seemed to bring out in him. Yet her expression as she sat opposite him was so sad it was all he could do not to offer comfort. The sort of comfort that could get him into all sorts of trouble. Curt had torn after the highly upset Darcy, now they were quite alone in Jock McIvor's study with McIvor's painted sapphire eyes checking on their every movement.

"I shouldn't have come," Courtney was saying mournfully, shaking her head as she replayed that upsetting scene.

"You answered your father's call," Adam offered smoothly, wondering where all these upsurges of suspicion were coming from. He certainly didn't have the old cliché blonde bimbo in mind—one couldn't miss her intelligence—it was just Ms. Courtney McIvor seemed to him the sort of young woman against whom a man needed a powerful defence.

Courtney as it happened was well aware of the undercurrents. She drew herself erect, staring across the desk into Adam's dark eyes. Surely there was a sparkle of mockery in their depths?

"He never mentioned the possibility of leaving you a great deal of money," Adam continued, "but you must have considered that was his clear intention?"

A chill entered Courtney's charming voice. "Strangely enough, Adam, my first thought as I've said before was seeing Darcy again."

"That's what decided you?" He focused on her face. Her skin was beautiful, without blemish. He doubted such a skin would stand up to Outback life. Not that she'd stay. She'd get what she came for and get out.

"I don't know why I'm repeating myself, but yes," she answered, sustaining the searching gaze.

"You never thought Darcy might consider you the enemy?"

Her eyes darkened. "I didn't think Darcy would hold what happened to us against me. I was a child. I had no option but to go with my mother."

"No doubt you'll want to get in touch with your mother?" He asked suavely. "Tell her the good news."

Courtney ignored that. "It seems however I've made an enemy out of you."

Adam backed off. "I'm sorry you should feel like that, Courtney, but I represent you *and* your sister."

Courtney answered promptly. "Who has Curt Berenger for a close friend. I don't think Curt is going to allow anyone to put anything over him, or Darcy. Curt and Darcy appear to have a troubled history but you saw his reaction. He really cares about her."

"He does." Adam inclined his dark head. "Your sister may well decide to fight the will. She did remain with her father all these years and it's universally accepted she lent him a great deal of support. There's also the fact your father led her to believe she would be the major beneficiary. That was how the first will was drafted."

Courtney could feel herself getting angry. "Darcy must do what she wants. She won't let me stand in her way. Besides, as far as I'm concerned, she won't have to fight anything. She can have whatever she wants. I waive any rights to my inheritance."

Adam kept his eyes on her. It was difficult not to she presented such an enchanting picture. "In any case we're talking at least eighty million." He heard her sucked in breath. "Maybe more. In other words, plenty to go around."

Her golden head snapped up. "I don't like you, Adam Maynard."

"You're kidding me," he smiled.

"No." She shook her head.

"You object to my being strictly factual?"

"I object to your questioning my motivation in coming here. I object to your unspoken insinuations I tried my hardest to exert influence over my father during his last days."

"And did you?" he asked quietly.

"I did *not.*" Courtney felt the warmth of anger so keenly it licked along her veins.

"But that's how it turned out?" he prompted in his lawyer's voice.

She should have expected this from Maynard. "It's one of the strange paradoxes of life, Adam. Surely you've encountered it in your career. Dying people make unexpected wills."

"Isn't that the truth!" Adam's slow smile lit his faintly severe face. "I suppose we'll never know."

"Know what?"

He shrugged. "Why exactly your father did it when all along he was emphatic Darcy would get the lion's share."

Courtney forced herself to remain calm. "I assure you I'm as much in shock as anyone. I did not take advantage of the situation as you seem to think. Exerting undue influence did not cross my mind."

"Of course not," he rejoined. "It was a potent combination of your youth, your beauty and your charm of manner." *Especially those big blue eyes,* he thought. *They'd hold any man's attention.* "Clearly Darcy is bitterly upset and disappointed."

Courtney nibbled her bottom lip. "Darcy loved Father a lot. He might not have been everyone's cup of tea but he must have been good to Darcy."

Oh good one, Adam thought but remained silent.

"He'd promised her she'd be rewarded for her love and loyalty. She must feel betrayed."

A steely light entered Adam's eyes. "Who could blame her for taking that view?"

Courtney felt like flinging a paper weight at him. "Look, I really don't need this. I'll renounce my rights. Today if you like."

"I don't think you should. I don't think you *will!*" he replied.

Courtney's small nostrils flared as anger flowed through her. She stood up in one swift movement, walking to the door. "Something I would like to do is change *you* as trustee."

His self-contained face remained impassive. "In which case the other trustees and your sister would have to agree. Curt trusts me. I believe Darcy does too. I'm sorry if I've offended you, Courtney, but it's my business to know everything. That includes the past."

She stared at him for several seconds. "If you're talking about *my* past I thought it was an open book?"

"Not at all!" He shrugged. "You told your father there was no-one, no *man* in your life—"

"How do you know that?" Courtney was taken aback.

"Because your father said so. One of his main concerns was that you didn't get involved with a man who took too great an interest in your money."

"I'm going for a walk." Courtney said defiantly, her *blue* eyes sparkling with resentment.

"May I join you?" Adam stood up, lean and elegant.

"Sorry, no. You raise my blood pressure. And it's only going to get worse."

"But I was so looking forward to it." He joined her at the door, his *dark* gaze locking on hers. "Tell me, do you remember much about the station?"

"I left it when I was ten." There was sarcasm in the way she said it.

"I can remember lots of things before I was ten," he said,

starting along the corridor so confidently, despite herself she felt compelled to fall into line.

"I suppose you'd already decided to get your teeth into law?" she suggested tartly.

"Not when I was that young," he said. When he spoke again his voice had subtly altered. "I thought I might become a firefighter."

"A firefighter?" She lifted her head in surprise. "A dangerous job when you're such a cautious man."

His expression suggested what he was going to say wasn't easy or even planned. "I was staying with my parents at our weekend retreat in the country," he said, dragging it out as though he was falling back on memory. "It was an old avocado plantation. During the night, the most terrifying night of my life, the old timber house caught fire. Dad rescued my mother and me and our two Labradors. *He* didn't get out himself."

Courtney was so shocked she stopped walking. She looked up at him in distress. "I am so sorry, Adam." She could only visualize the horror of the night. The dreadful memories he'd never get out of his system even if he lived forever.

Instantly his face that had been charged with feeling assumed its habitual mask. "I don't know why I told you that."

"Do you think it was a mistake?"

He continued to stare into her eyes. "I haven't spoken about it in many years." It had to be some special knack she had. Her spell had worked on her father.

"It must have been a horrendous experience for you and your mother," she said with exquisite gentleness.

"My mother couldn't handle it." His answer was tense. "Dad was her life. I was reared by my paternal grandparents."

Courtney couldn't ignore the implication. "Does that mean?"

He appeared to look down and right through her. "The one thing I can't talk about, Courtney. No more questions, please." He recommenced walking.

Courtney followed, unable to conceal her shock. Adam Maynard maybe thirty was already a partner in a prestigious law firm. He looked and spoke as though he had been born with every advantage in life yet he had known terrible tragedy. "Would you like me to drive you around the station?" she offered in a voice that was tender with sympathy. "I do remember a lot of things as it happens. I should be able to point out a few landmarks. I think we should leave Darcy and Curt a note before we go. They'll wonder if they find us gone."

He hesitated, only briefly. "Thank you, Courtney. I'd like that. One moment and I'll see to it." He turned to walk back to the study for pen and paper.

"Leave the note on the console in the entrance hall," she suggested. "They'll see it there. I'll wait for you on the verandah."

He was continually amazed by the size of the Outback skies, so brilliantly cloudlessly *blue.* This was a vast land. Surreal in its way. A savage wilderness that was nevertheless unbelievably dramatic. And *dazzling!* Not just the quality of light that played tricks on perspective, but the vivid baked-in ochres of the terrain, the colours used by aboriginal artists some of whom were receiving world acclaim: the oranges and bright yellows, the burning reds, the stark whites, the cobalts, the mauves and the amethysts.

With every trip he was becoming more and more sensitive to the land's primal splendour and its changing moods. Across the quivering Spinifex plains phantom hills thrust up towards the sky, long enticing chains of billabongs at their feet. This was a fascinating region, a riverine desert, irrigated by a maze of waterways that ran into three great rivers, the Diamantina, the Georgina and Cooper's Creek which in turn flowed into the inland sea of salt, *Katitanda,* Lake Eyre in the remote desert lands. The desert tribes feared Katitanda and never went near it.

For most of the way—they had been travelling for about

thirty minutes—the two of them were silent each seemingly lost in their own thoughts. Now Courtney pointed to a line of sandstone hills that as they approached began to go through the alluring colour changes that were so unique to the Interior. The bluish-purple turned to salmon pink then closer to fiery red.

Fascinating! Adam was captivated by the wonders of nature.

"Have you ever seen our rock paintings?" Courtney asked.

"To be honest, Courtney, I didn't know Murraree had any. I know about the galleries on Sunset Downs."

She nodded, expertly steering the jeep across rough ground, littered with polished gibbers that sparkled in the sun. "Of course I've seen those when I was small, but I don't really remember. Some station owners like to keep the galleries secret if only to protect them. Sunset's are more important than ours. Would you like to take a look? I should warn you. It's not easygoing."

He couldn't prevent a laugh escaping. "Then how are *you* going to manage?" He was visualizing her petite dancer's body climbing the rock face. At university he'd been a top athlete, track and field, but he didn't tell her that.

"I'm a lot tougher than I look," she replied composedly. "I was born here, not that I was wonderfully athletic like Darcy. There was nothing she couldn't do. I expect you've heard I was terrified of horses. Still am. Not *terrified* exactly but I like to keep my distance."

"I expect your father didn't handle you as sensitively as a father should," he said dryly.

"Gosh no!" Courtney shuddered in memory. Some things one never forgot. Her father she often thought at such times had to be mad. "He threw Darcy on a horse and she rode. He tried to do the same with me and I screamed and screamed. Horses are so *big* and dangerous and so unpredictable. I remember some pretty wild ones."

"I could teach you how to ride if we had the time," he said, his tone casual.

Courtney turned her golden head in surprise. "You can ride?" He looked the ultimate sophisticated city slicker.

His brilliant eyes mocked. "I can ride as well as I can walk. My grandparents owned a pastoral property in Central Queensland. Sheep and cattle. Not a vast station like you have here in the Channel Country but big enough to get in a lot of riding."

"Well, well, opportunity knocks!" she laughed. "Are your grandparents still alive?" Courtney turned her head briefly. It felt strange to be in such close proximity to him. Strange and a little scary. Exciting too. This man she knew would give her no quarter.

"No, Courtney, I'm an orphan." His expressive voice was a touch hard.

"So you've experienced a lot of sorrow?"

"And a lot of love." He gave another one of his elegant shrugs. "My grandparents were very cherishing and protective. I loved them dearly. I guess my grandfather wanted me to take over the farm but he could see I needed to spread my wings. I was a good student. I did well. I decided on the law."

"Are you glad? Do you find it fulfilling?" She allowed her blue eyes to touch on his profile. Good forehead, good nose, good chin. His story had touched on her heart.

"Yes and no," he murmured. "Sometimes practising law can be a dirty business. Your job is to look after the client. The richer the client the harder the job. The rich can be very greedy. They don't like to part with their money. It's my job to help them hold on to as much of it as possible and still keep within the letter of the law."

"Sounds like you don't admire a lot of them?"

"Sometimes I don't admire myself," he said wryly. "One or two I'd like to kick out and tell them I don't want their blasted work."

"I can understand that. It must be a battle to keep them honest. Curt said you have a splendid financial brain."

He turned his *dark* head, giving her such a mocking look she sucked in her breath. "I'll look after you and your sister, Courtney."

"Surely you want this work?" she asked a shade tartly.

"Yes I do, though it was more or less Curt who got me the job. Your father didn't like me."

"Maybe you made him feel uneasy," she replied. "It's no secret my father was a rogue. The *only* one in the family I might add." She pressed the *only* home.

CHAPTER SIX

THOUGH she and her flat-mate Lisa attended a gym a couple of times a week, Courtney was unashamedly puffing by the time they'd reached the first line of sandstone caves. She had to blink rapidly to keep the sweat out of her eyes. He on the other hand had climbed as lightly and skilfully as a mountain goat. Now he stood above her like Hillary at the summit of Everest, offering a hand.

"I suppose you expect me to say thank you," she panted, so close to him she had to grasp the front of his shirt. "You're doing it on purpose aren't you?"

"Doing what?" He stared down into her enchanting face, flushed like a rose. "It was your idea, Courtney. I've taken it as slowly as I could."

"For *my* sake, you mean. Heck, let's get out of the sun. It could burn a hole right through me."

"Do you know where you're going?" he asked mildly enough though it struck her as sarcastic.

"Sure I do," she lied. Though any goose could find the hill country in thousands of kilometres of open plain, the rugged terrain was nowhere near as familiar as she had imagined. It was almost time to face it. She wasn't sure where they were. *Precisely.* Heavens she'd only been ten when she left. And not an adventurous ten either. Her father had seen to that.

Maynard was wearing one of her father's collection of akubras and he looked sickeningly good looking, like a professional hunter out on safari. She dragged her eyes away from him looking fixedly ahead. "See that cave opening left of centre?" She played a hunch. "The one with the tree growing out of the rock face."

"The yellow flowers?" he questioned. Even as he spoke some gorgeous little birds arrived with fluttering wings, thrusting their beaks into the fluffy yellow balls.

"I'm almost certain that's one of them." She wasn't. The red cliff face stretched up and away like the ruins of an ancient civilisation. Thousands of building blocks glowed orange and red and salmon pink. They appeared unbroken on either side except for some horizontal cave openings that could prove to be deep or shallow.

"And how do we go about avoiding snakes?" he asked, turning to question her. "Isn't this the land of the reptiles, large dangerous snakes and alarming lizards?"

"Look," she said kindly, "the lizards might look alarming but except for the big goannas they're quite harmless. As for the snakes, you're a man. You do something."

"Right." He bent to picked up a stout stick that was lying on the rocky ground and brandished it. "I'm no Indiana Jones."

"Actually he was frightened of snakes too." She had seen all the Indiana Jones movies.

"If I rescue you I might have to charge," he warned her. "I'm a lawyer, don't forget."

For a lawyer he looked pretty darn good in the Great Outdoors she thought wryly grateful he took the lead. He was laughing at her. Of course he was, the conceited so and so. On her mettle, Courtney scrambled after him, regretting she was no Darcy, but he laid a restraining hand on her arm. "Steady. We won't rush into it. Surely rock wallabies take shelter in these caves?"

"Anyone would think it was a lion!" Impulsively she

started forward, trying to prove she was a McIvor when a split second later an animal flew at her from out of the cave. It was snarling ferociously, yellow coat bristling, eyes golden in the dazzling sunlight.

"Hell!" Adam breathed harshly, putting himself with remarkable speed between Courtney and the vicious predator. With one arm he swung her out of the way. She went down like a doll, legs collapsing inelegantly under her, scraping an elbow on the jumble of sharp stones.

"Get!" Adam yelled at the snarling menace, swinging the branch at the dingo that looked like it was about to charge and fasten its teeth into some point on Adam's long legs. He stood his ground, fixing those yellow luminous eyes with a glare of his own. "Go on, get. Scat!"

It was obvious the cunning wild dog was in two minds. It continued to snarl, at close range a frightening and dangerous opponent. It was only a foot away muscles bunched, then seemingly in answer to Courtney's frenzied prayers, it abruptly backed up, skidded, righted itself, then took off like a rocket. Its fast passage threw up stones and red dust until it reached the plain where it continued its mad flight. Adam helped it on its way by pelting the branch after it, his aim so accurate it hit the dingo's flanks.

"I wonder if it's got mates," he said tersely, turning to jerk Courtney to her feet. "That was damned silly! Have you hurt yourself?"

She gave a little wail. "A bit of wounded pride, I think."

"Show me that." He examined her scraped elbow. "Well there is a saying: Pride comes before the fall. That wants cleaning and some antiseptic."

"I'll live." She made a face. "Don't tell Darcy okay?"

He smiled, his dark face suddenly full of light. "You're fine. You didn't cry."

Her antipathy returned. "What's that supposed to mean?"

He studied her face lingeringly, something that thoroughly disconcerted and exhilarated her at one and the same time. "Not much, Courtney." He hunched a shoulder so elegantly she began to wonder if he had French blood. "Just a passing remark."

"Someone told you I used to cry a lot when I was a little girl?" she questioned in an aggrieved tone.

"So what? When your father's idea of fun was throwing you up screaming onto the back of a horse? Well that's it, we better go back."

She brought her hands to her hips. "Where's your sense of adventure? We've only just arrived. That was quite a climb even if you didn't feel it. You're not apprehensive about meeting up with another dingo, are you?"

"I'd be a fool if I weren't," he clipped off. "I've never seen any dog so menacing even pit bull terriers. Dingoes are killers. The truth is, I don't want any more harm to come to *you,* Courtney."

"I thought you already had me cast as a troublemaker?" She gave him a challenging look.

"Maybe it's going to take me a little while to realize how truly innocent you are. Now, if you're hell-bent on seeing whether or not you've led us on a wild-goose chase, which I'm beginning to think is a distinct possibility, I'll take a look inside. *You* stay here."

"Take care you don't bump your head," she called sweetly, giving in to the temptation to taunt.

"At least that won't happen to you," he returned.

Smartass! It would be wonderful to grow another couple of inches. Short people were taken less seriously. She watched him bend his dark head slouch his shoulders, then disappear into the mouth of the cave.

Moments passed. She began to feel alarm. Let's face it, she'd sent him in there. He might meet with some harm and it would be her fault. If so she hadn't meant it. The trip had started out to offer comfort and conciliation after his tragic disclosure.

"Adam?" she called, sniffing the air for animal scent and staring into the cave. "Are you okay in there?"

Silence.

Had something awful happened? For some reason she started to think of the famous Australian story Picnic at Hanging Rock that had been made into a movie where a number of school girls had disappeared into a cave never to be seen again. Hard to think that would happen to a hard nosed, super efficient lawyer like Adam Maynard who was turning out to be rather amazing.

She sank down a little and ventured into the cave. "Adam?" She heard the quiver in her voice. This was insane! He couldn't just disappear.

A hard muscular arm came around her. Held her tight. "You were a damned long time coming."

She collapsed against him like a souffle, feeling the thrill and the danger. At close range Adam Maynard was lethal. "Why didn't you answer?" She gritted. Given she didn't like the man it was bizarre how being locked in his arms turned her on.

"I wanted to see if you'd come in after me or hotfoot it home," he said bending his head until his mouth was close to her ear. Her hair and her skin, her whole body gave off the scent of wildflowers.

"Only a worm would say a thing like that! You think I'm a coward?" She spun, ready to do battle only her eyes had become adjusted to the gloom. "Oh goodness!" she broke off, hostility forgotten. Still cocooned in his arms she lifted her marvelling gaze to the ceiling. "I told you. Isn't this wonderful? And *I* found it."

"All the more incredible because I'm sure it was a fluke," he murmured, a mocking smile on his lips.

She ignored him. "I'm absolutely certain I've never been in this cave before. I've never seen those rock drawings."

"Well we've got *that* sorted out. They're extraordinary, aren't they?"

"Oh yes!" she whispered, craning her neck. "Darcy must know about them."

"She probably does, although there must be hundreds of caves in this area. A lot could be galleries. I read somewhere they could run to tens of thousands over the country which means there must be hundreds of sites not yet seen or recorded. Some of them could be extremely important."

"Exactly. Listen…are you going to let me go?" she enquired sweetly, shifting her gaze to his face.

"What man in his right mind wouldn't let you nestle against him?" he responded, although he dropped his arms immediately. "It's amazing, Courtney, how very enchanting you are."

"That sounds more than a tad sarcastic," she said, flushing and moving away. Next he'd accuse her of trying to seduce him.

Courtney began to wander about the softly glowing interior. The floor of the cave was yellow sand imprinted with the footsteps of small creatures. "I don't have a clue what they mean though I can spot the mythical beings and over there the hunters with their spears."

"That can't be a crocodile in the middle of the desert," Adam examined an incised drawing.

"Sure looks like one," Courtney said drolly, daring to return to his side. "The kangaroos are ten times as big. Giants. Maybe they're dinosaurs. They found the fossilized bones of a huge dinosaur not all that far from here." The paintings were executed in ochres, red, yellow, white, black, a dark charcoal. The ceiling was covered and two walls. "Look, Adam, that's a fishing scene and those are turtles." She took care not to pollute the drawings with her hands.

"Such a wealth of aboriginal culture!" he murmured, pondering the drawings. "These drawings must be incredibly old."

"Yet the colours are so bright you'd think no one had ever seen them or disturbed them."

"Apart from the likes of our dingo friend and a few assorted lizards and snakes."

All in all the cave was a mass of drawings. To Courtney's mind they gave off a curious *energy.* There were stick people in hunting scenes, mammals, birds, fish, what appeared to be a crocodile and the long undulating outlines of many snakes including the legendary Rainbow Snake.

"This is quite an experience," Adam said, after they had given the cave a total inspection. "What's the betting we can find it again?"

He was wearing that mocking smile again. "As far as I'm concerned, you're a dark horse, Adam Maynard," she said. "I had you pinned as a city slicker but I bet you know your way around the bush."

He made a mock bow. "That depends on whether I'm following *you* or not, Courtney. You're a wonderful guide and it's not just your driving."

"I'm a good driver," she bristled. "I've never lost a single point."

"Congratulations. Me neither. But then I'm a lawyer. Lawyers have to be on their best behaviour. Especially when they're *your* lawyer."

"When you're really yearning to be something different," she said quietly

There was a short somewhat charged silence. "Ah, you've found me out."

"Just a thought." His brilliant gaze made her restless. "You've no wife to worry about."

"A huge saving!" His voice was infuriatingly sardonic. "I've seen too many people make mistakes and pay for it. Which is not to say any day now I couldn't find myself madly in love."

"I doubt that will happen," Courtney eyed him critically. "You're too comfortable with yourself. And your skills."

"Nothing I'm sure a good woman couldn't change."

His eyes rested on her. In the heat her gilded curls clung to her scalp, emphasizing the perfect shape of her skull. The glow within the cave lent her skin a pearl like luminescence. It would be difficult indeed for any man to resist her charms, he thought soberly. He found himself understanding how her father had derived such comfort from her presence. Had she worked it that way? The last *light* he saw. There were so many questions that would never be answered.

You know what you've got to do. A voice inside his head said. *You have to get out of here before some kind of madness overtakes you. Remember your position of trust and responsibility.*

Adam took her arm lightly, on the surface utterly self-possessed, but his fingers had a life of their own. For a mere instant they traced her creamy skin, savouring the satiny texture.

Courtney's breath caught. Her blood turned to steam. She hadn't planned on anything like this. Events were slipping beyond her control. She didn't like that. No less than her sister she had been strongly influenced by her parents' traumatic breakup.

"I suppose we'd better go back before I start to tell you how lovely you are."

His tone seemed to taunt her. Of course he was testing her in some way. Setting little traps. She took a moment to answer. "I expect I'll be hearing a lot of that from now on. After all, I'm an heiress, aren't I?"

"Absolutely," he assured her suavely. "Unless you stick to your vow to renounce your inheritance. Or have you forgotten?"

"I have the good sense to know you're baiting me," Courtney said. "What I would suggest is you trust me."

It was clear from his dark brooding gaze he did not.

CHAPTER SEVEN

COURTNEY moved into the kitchen looking around the huge room which had been sadly neglected. Except for a few token gestures towards modernity it looked pretty much as it must have looked in her grandfather's day. The old kitchen block built in colonial times was a little distance from the main house across a very pleasant courtyard. That was the custom then, offering insulation against possible fire damage, heat and the activities of the servants. She and Darcy had played in the old kitchen block when they were little. When the *new* kitchen had been installed the massive range and the bread oven had been salvaged and brought into the house. It was still in splendid working order. In fact it would be ideal for cooking huge quantities of food say for an army, Courtney thought. As it was there was only McIvor and Darcy rattling around a huge house. McIvor had fired Mrs. Andersen who had been Murraree's housekeeper in their childhood because Mrs. Andersen had been loyal to their mother and foolish enough to show it.

There had been no housekeeper since. The homestead desperately needed one and other staff possibly two or three girls living on the station who would be grateful for the training and the money. Darcy must have had a rugged time of it, Courtney considered with a great pang of guilt. She must have taken over the cooking and all the domestic duties except for the years she had been sent away to boarding school. McIvor probably had his women visit then to look after him. Multimillionaire he might have been but he obviously loathed spending money on what he considered inessentials. The entire homestead was desperately in need of renovation and refurbishing. It struck her she would love to do it.

She was examining all the old cupboards and shelves when Darcy pranced into the room like a high stepping filly. To Courtney it reaffirmed her sister's childhood athleticism. And of course there was the outdoor life style.

"There you are!" Darcy's eyes. her most remarkable feature, were like aquamarine chips.

"I was just thinking the kitchen could do with some updating," Courtney ventured. "Those shelves for instance could look very attractive if they were painted and lined with some of the beautiful china that's been stashed away."

For some reason Darcy felt hurt. "I've wanted to do lots of things, Courtney, but Dad had to think long and hard about spending money on the homestead. I couldn't nag him."

"Goodness, I know you couldn't," Courtney well remembered her father's aggressive nature. "But he's left us now."

"And doesn't the house feel empty," Darcy moaned, pulling out a kitchen chair and slumping into it. "Why did I love him so, Courtney?" she asked as though she desperately needed someone to explain it to her. "I see now he didn't really concern himself with me. Love was just another four letter word to Dad."

There was a good deal of evidence for that. "Then he missed out on so much," Courtney said with real sadness. "For us women, love is the focus of our lives. Father was all you had." Courtney dearly wanted to give comfort, but she knew Darcy demanded her own space.

"You were gone a while with Adam?" Abruptly Darcy lifted her head. Something about her sister's exquisite appearance had decided Darcy against her habitual plait. She wore her hair caught at the nape with a distinctive gold clasp she'd found tucked away in a drawer. Probably one of her grandmother's. "What do you think of him?" she asked, aware there was a charge in the atmosphere around Adam and her sister. Hostility might have been wrong. But it was something not far from it.

Courtney hesitated a moment. "To be honest, I don't know what to think of him. He's a very challenging man. A complex one too. What I *do* think however is, he will look after our interests well."

"Our interests!" Darcy scoffed, eyes flashing. "They're both waiting for me to settle down before they start giving it to us straight. Probably after dinner. They've had their heads together most of the afternoon. I hope you realize we're more or less at their mercy?"

"Surely you trust Curt?" Courtney asked, wondering what the *exact* relationship was between Curt Berenger and her sister. Both seemed to rank very high on the other's agenda. "Would you like a cup of coffee?" She felt like one herself.

"Yes, thanks." Darcy nodded absently. "I trust him. Of course I do but I have lots of feelings of anger."

"Are you angry at me?" Courtney paused in what she was doing, knowing she would be terribly distressed if Darcy said, yes.

Darcy gave a deep sigh. "I was, Courtney, but I have a huge struggle trying to overcome the love I had for you when we were kids. It's not easy for me to hate. But for *years* I've felt utterly alienated. But now you're here!" She threw up a helpless hand. A hand which Courtney reached out to catch, thinking physical contact was important.

"We're sisters, Darcy. We're family. However much we've both been hurt I never stopped loving you. Nor did Mum."

Instantly Darcy withdrew her hand. "My feelings for you don't extend to our mother," she said bluntly. "She saved herself at my expense. And what am I now? I'll tell you. I'm a tall thin woman who doesn't spend enough time looking after herself. This is a tough environment, Courtney. I've worked very hard. Dad thought it perfectly natural, so I did too. I've neglected the house, I know. I couldn't get around it all. I might be waging a war against Curt at the moment—he thinks simply for the hell of it—but he's right, I can't run Murraree on my own. It needs a man."

"A man like Curt," Courtney supplied, placed a cup of coffee at her sister's hand.

"You like him, don't you?" Darcy made herself search her sister's guileless blue eyes.

"Sure I do!" Courtney smiled. "To me he's a prince. I wouldn't let him get away if I were you."

Darcy didn't shift her gaze. "What's to stop *you* going after him?" she asked.

"You're kidding!" Courtney made a little jeering sound. "Do you have any idea how unlikely that is? I'm not the McIvor woman Curt is interested in. I never was. I never will be. But I'd love him for a brother-in-law."

"That's not about to happen." Darcy felt almost light-headed with relief.

"Why not? Why can't you deal with it? Is there anything I can do to help?"

"I'm a mess, Courtney," Darcy said, wishing she knew her sister better so she could confide in her.

"No you're not." Courtney's tender heart twisted with pain. "Don't lose him, Darcy. What ever is in the way, I have a feeling *you're* the one who has to kick down the barrier."

Except in doing so she could find herself alienated again. It was all so sad. In retrospect Darcy realized she should have had it out with Curt at the time, only then she had found it impossible. "Have you ever been in love?" she asked her sister wistfully.

Courtney stared at her for a moment. "I thought I was once. It didn't last."

"Do you know how many marriages end in divorce?" Darcy finished off her coffee. "It's at least half."

"Divorce, ugly divorce is always in my mind too, Darcy. It's because of Mum and Dad. Not all marriages turn out like that. Mum is happily married to Peter. Most of my friend's parents are happily married."

"Would they tell you if they weren't?" Darcy challenged, her tone suddenly cynical. "McIvor must have been in love with our mother at the beginning."

"She would have been very very, pretty," Courtney said. "Still is. McIvor attached a lot of importance to a woman's looks. But being *in* love isn't a strong enough anchor. They didn't share or grow together. They didn't even laugh together. Mum couldn't handle all his philandering. Come to that, I couldn't handle a husband's philandering either, though many women do. Before I marry I want to be very, very sure."

"Even then it's a risk." Darcy sounded as though she felt unable to attempt it herself.

"You must take lots of risks around the station," Courtney said bracingly. "I know you've got your pilot's licence and you can fly a helicopter. Some people would consider that a risky accomplishment."

Darcy nodded, focusing on what her sister was saying. "You know Curt's father was killed when a chopper came down on Sunset? They'd been out on muster. Mr. Berenger was a passenger.The pilot was a very experienced man."

"I heard about it," Courtney said. "That must have been terrible."

"It was." A shiver passed through Darcy's slender body. "Philip Berenger was a wonderful man. The family and all their many friends were devastated. Even Dad was terribly upset. He looked on Mr. Berenger as a man of integrity. That's why he hit on Curt as executor and trustee of his will. There are many risks in our way of life. No getting away from it. But risks of the heart are something else again. As we discovered when parents make mistakes the children pay."

Courtney put out a hand. "Would you see, Mum, some time, Darcy?" she pleaded. "She's desperate to see you."

Darcy's eyes glinted. "I don't share your love and loyalty, Courtney. I'm not ready to resume any relationship with her. Please don't ask again."

Courtney's fair skin coloured. "I'm sorry. I respect your feelings."

"I don't think you do. Why didn't you tell me you'd seen Curt and his mother over the years?"

Now Courtney paled. "So you know about that?"

"I confronted Curt with it," Darcy explained, her voice edgy. "You and he simply didn't greet one another like long lost friends. I had it out with him."

"Try to forgive us," Courtney begged. "Mum was too fearful of what Father would do. Being very rich can give a person authority over others. Mum anticipated turmoil if you were brought back into our world. She was frightened you'd rebel, even run away. She was convinced Dad would come after you. It's a course of action that fits the man. Even Mrs Berenger thought telling you would create more problems than it would solve. Aggression was part of our father's personality."

Darcy couldn't deny it. She had seen many instances of that. Mercifully never directed against herself but active with station staff or anyone who angered him. McIvor's identity was all tied up with being a law unto himself.

She sighed deeply. "Well it's a defence I suppose, Courtney, but it doesn't disguise the fact you all lied to me. Just how many lies am I supposed to survive?"

Courtney's eyes shimmered with tears. "I solemnly swear

I'll never mislead you again. You're back in my life, Darcy. I can't lose you. I want to give support to you in every way. The path our parents took wasn't of our choosing."

"Okay, okay!" Darcy held up a restraining hand, though she was deeply affected by her sister's tears. "Let's get off such a painful subject. What are we going to give the men for dinner?"

Courtney dashed a hand across her eyes. She stood up and went to the refrigerator, putting her head into it. "Steak and salad?" she suggested, huskily. "The steak's superb."

"It certainly is." Darcy smiled with satisfaction. "Murraree beef."

Courtney opened the freezer door. "And there's plenty of ice cream."

"Tinned peaches, pears, plums, fruit salad you name it in the pantry. I loathe cooking. I never learned to be domesticated."

"I'd loathe it too if I had to work in this kitchen." Courtney pulled a little face. "Actually I love cooking. Mum and I used to go along to classes." As soon as she said it she could have bitten her tongue.

"How nice for you." Sarcasm rose off Darcy like heat waves. "Like I said, Courtney, she might have been a first class mother to you, but she threw me to the lions."

Darcy was amazed at how attractive Courtney had made what she and her father had called The Breakfast Room. Not that they'd breakfasted there. They had always eaten a quick breakfast at the huge kitchen table. The Breakfast Room was right off the kitchen allowing Courtney to go to and fro with ease.

From somewhere she had found a crisply starched white linen and lace tablecloth, matching napkins, an elegant white bone china dinner set with a gold rim and a gold medallion in the centre of the plates, silver cutlery, two beautiful silver candlesticks complete with candles, and to top it all off, assembled a centre arrangement comprising very simple things; a froth of cerise bouganvillea offset by some shiny dark green leaves. The low ceramic container had an attractive gold feature. Darcy was sure she had never seen it before in her life.

There was an eye catching arrangement on the sideboard as well. Cactus leaves of all things and a magnificent banksias in yet another unusual container. She would have to ask Courtney where she had found them. Not that there weren't innumerable unopened cupboards. Courtney was just so clever! In comparison Darcy felt a positive hick.

The food was just as good. In fact it was the best meal Darcy had had in quite a while. For a starter Courtney had concocted a stack of tomato, mozzarella and basil with a great vinaigrette. Balsamic vinegar and lime? There were limes and lemons in a basket in the kitchen. The steaks were pan seared accompanied by vegetables from the refrigerator, rounds of yellow and green courgettes garnished with cherry tomatoes and spring onions. For dessert she had assembled a colourful tropical fruit salad from the selection of tins in the pantry, spiked it with something, cointreau? serving it with whipped cream and ice cream. It was quite a coup given there hadn't been a great deal of anything to work with.

Except the wine. A wine connoisseur would have been on cloud nine. McIvor hadn't worried where the pennies went when it came to stocking the cellar. Down beneath the house, there were rows and rows of vintage reds, chardonnays and rieslings, champagnes, dessert wines label to label. Gallons of spirits especially the finest Scotch whisky of which McIvor had been inordinately fond.

Such an excellent meal with splendid wines gave the conversation a kick start. It flourished. Not much of a drinker, as if McIvor would have allowed such a thing, Darcy rolled the stem of her wineglass between two fingers as she watched her sister interact with the two men. Courtney's golden hair gleamed like a halo, her cheeks were flushed with rose accentuating the perfection of her skin and the blue of her eyes. She wore a very pretty halter necked dress in a pinky mauve and as the neckline dipped you could see the upward swell of her creamy breasts. Courtney looked, her sister considered, good enough to eat.

The men obviously thought so too. They were looking very happy with their lot, all praise and attention. As well they might be. It seemed to Darcy as she continued to observe, Courtney had more than a little of not her mother's but her father's sexual magnetism.

At a momentary lull in the conversation Curt turned his wide shoulders and looked full into Darcy's face. "You've gone quiet?"

"Preparing myself for what lies ahead," she said dryly. "That was a beautiful meal, Courtney," she said sincerely. "Thank you so much."

"Hear, hear!" Both men raised their glasses to salute the domestic goddess.

"Now you sit here and I'll take care of the rest." Darcy who had been pleased to have been kept out of the kitchen thought it was squarely her turn.

"I won't hear of it." Courtney smiled.

Darcy was firm. "I insist."

"Didn't you promise I could help, Darcy?" Curt sat back smiling.

"I don't need help, thank you," Darcy returned sweetly.

"Oh yes you do!" In one lithe movement he rose to his feet. A marvellous looking man. "Besides you're a little tiddly."

"As if!" Darcy muttered, thinking of her wayward father.

"Have it your own way. Let's just *do* it." Curt began to load plates onto the three tiered timber and steel trolley. "Courtney and Adam can enjoy the night air. The stars are out in all their glory."

"We have to stop meeting like this," he joked, when they were behind the closed kitchen door. "I think I'm falling in love with Courtney. She's a good inventive cook and she knows how to present things."

Darcy shot a quick sideways glance at him, forced to consider Curt was a free man. "Not to mention herself. She's lovely. Could you be interested?" She didn't think Courtney would stand a chance if Curt turned his attention on her.

He laughed, looking genuinely amused. "Darcy, to me she's still a little kid in a way. A very pretty little kid. Your sister." His expression was indulgent.

"And she's witty and charming," Darcy persisted, all sorts of ideas circulating in her head.

"What else does a woman need?" Curt responded nonchalantly. "I'll wipe. You wash. Why in tarnation don't you have a dish washer? I thought everyone—but everyone—had one."

"I can manage dishes you know," Darcy said feeling she had to defend herself in some way. "I tried to give Dad the right foods but in the last few years he swore off fruit and vegetables. He was a beef, bacon, and potatoes man washed down with a couple of bottles of red wine. It just struck me he used to get bitterly sarcastic afterwards."

"I do recall," Curt said dryly. "I'm sure if you had a proper medical they'd find rocks in your head."

"Thank you," said Darcy. She gave a deep sigh. "I've been a terrible fool haven't I, Curt?"

He didn't answer but started to whistle tunelessly. He took out a couple of clean tea towels. "One day if you're a very good girl you're going to find Mr. Right, so you mustn't get maudlin. By the way I love you in a dress. How many have you actually got?" She was wearing a simple summer dress which her delicate height managed to turn into elegance.

"Maybe a hundred," she said, forcing flippancy. "All designer label, all very very expensive. You know I don't get much opportunity for wearing dresses, Curt."

"Invent them," he suggested standing off a little to survey her. "You've no idea what a change it makes from your usual gear."

She flicked suds at him. "It must be Courtney's influence. She's started me thinking." In more ways than one.

"I'd love her for that alone," Curt said with such feeling it further confused her. "That's a beautiful clasp you've got in your hair but it would look better out." With a deft movement so characteristic of him he undid the gold clasp and put it down on the table."

"Now see what you've gone and done," Darcy cried, as her thick gleaming hair fell all around her face. "I can hardly see the dishes."

"Here, let me." Sensing she was emotional he took over.

"It's so funny to see you washing up," Darcy managed after a little while. "The great Curt Berenger. I'd love your polo team to see you now."

"Who would care!" He slipped another dish into the rack. "I'm not above doing the washing up now and again."

"You mean on the occasions you come over here?" she asked wryly.

"Your father always made sure he was in attendance."

"Didn't he now!" she said in a voice that broke.

"He was terrified of losing you." Curt finished off the last dish then wiped his hands. "That would well and truly have broken his pride. Hey, you're not crying, are you?" There was much concern in his voice.

"I'm definitely not crying." She turned her head away grateful her hair formed a protective veil.

"Then look at me. I was only teasing, Darcy."

"I know," she murmured bleakly.

He turned her back towards him, tilting her chin. "You'll get past all this trauma. You'll lead a wider life. You're brave and strong. You're beautiful too. So beautiful." He took her face in his hands, his voice like black velvet. "Kiss me. I'm not moving until you do."

Heat flushed through her body. "Someone might come," she warned, staring back over her shoulder as though Courtney and Adam were about to beat down the kitchen door.

"Easy, Darcy! Let them come. You're not getting off."

She could feel the naked electricity crackling between them. Enough to light up a town. "That's a threat?"

"No threats. A challenge." His voice mocked, but the expression in his eyes made her heart flutter violently.

"Then a kiss you shall have." Incredibly she answered, her blood filled with sparks. "But a quick one."

"Can you make it last five or six hours?"

"No. It's not as though you don't know where these kisses lead." Despite that, knowing what she knew, she placed her hands upon his shoulders, feeling the warmth of his skin. She tilted her head, feeling the heavy silk of her hair afloat against her nape. His hands were moving so slowly down her back, pressing her against him. The excitement was mounting with every moment. Frantic energy. Yet her kiss was very gentle, as delicate as she could make it. Gossamer light. The tip of her tongue ranged over his lips, tracing the sensuous outline. Such a beautiful mouth he had. She remembered exactly *where* to place the kisses.

Again and again.

Bliss all around them, the scent of the exquisite native boronia, warm sand beneath them, sunlight falling in filigreed chinks through the thick screen of trees. Her heart doing backflips…

A man's voice. Curt's. His breath rasping in his throat.

"Oh, you're unpredictable, Darcy. What are you doing? Playing games?" He threw back his head so he could stare into her face.

"You used to like games?" she asked in a voice so seductive it couldn't possibly be hers. In reality it was fuelled by her anxiety Curt could become interested in her sister.

"So I did." His green eyes glowed like crystals. He lowered his head and this time *he* did the kissing.

She clung to him throughout, needing no other thing but him. His hands were clamped on her hips holding her lower body to him. They sizzled where they touched. Heat pouring from their skin.

The kiss grew deeper and deeper, drawing a little moan from her. She felt the ache in the pit of her stomach as muscles began to contract. His hand found the contours of her breast taking its soft weight. Desire began to weigh her down. Lovemaking like this called for a bed.

"Sleep with me," he muttered urgently. "I've had enough of memories."

Who knows what she would have answered if there hadn't been a distraction. She was coming inexorably to a major turning point in her life. It was time to explain what had driven them apart. Absolve him from his guilt.

Only from out of nowhere she heard Courtney's voice reverberating. "Well, not *me,* thank *you,* very much!"

She sounded angry.

"Bloody hell!" Curt groaned in frustration, coming out of his trance. He dropped his arms from around Darcy's slender body. "The tour of the garden obviously didn't go well."

"We'd better see what's the matter." Distractedly Darcy caught up the gold clasp and bundled her hair into it, aware long coils had escaped around her cheeks and her nape. "Have I any lipstick left?" she asked, flags of colour in her cheeks.

"The question isn't about lipstick," he gritted, "it's about having sex. You know, making love. I can't turn my feelings on and off like a tap, okay?" His eyes scintillated in a face taut with emotion. "It might take a little planning. No big deal.

No one will find out if you must continue to act the adolescent."

"That's cruel!" she panted, hearing her sister's voice again.

"Cruel or not, take my advice, Darcy." Curt looked like he wasn't prepared to take no for an answer. "Dive right in."

CHAPTER EIGHT

BOTH sisters sat on the edge of their chairs. Both looked and felt nerve ridden. Darcy with her personal life in crisis. Courtney angry with Adam Maynard who perversely attracted her. It was hard to believe her own treacherous feelings. She knew he was assessing her wrongly. Heaven knows she hadn't come here after her father's wretched money but when she'd got around to really thinking about it surely he owed her a sizeable chunk? Not half. Darcy deserved the lion's share, but a decent chunk. In no way had she unfairly wormed her way into McIvor's affections. No way! Courtney fumed.

Darcy, experiencing another primitive surge of feminism, studied the two impressive young men ranged opposite them. There they sat in all their masculine glory, supremely self-confident, both appearing quite unaffected by the tense atmosphere in the room. Adam had his legal face on. Curt breathed authority, splendid masculine common sense. Co-conspirators. Practically brothers.

McIvor, that born trouble maker, watched them all. There was even a twist to his smile Darcy thought. It was something she had just caught sight of.

"We'll pick up where we left off, shall we?" Adam asked, smiling at the unsmiling young women who looked both serious and challenging.

"No need to ease us into it, Adam," Darcy said. "All I ask is you make it quick and cut the legal terminology."

"Right." Adam began briskly

There was an air of total unreality about the whole thing. At one point Courtney's hand stole into her sister's. Darcy squeezed hard. Neither spoke until Adam had finished reading and explaining the terms of their father's will.

By that time Courtney's head was swimming. She left it to Darcy, the elder, who was trying hard to keep her emotions in check to speak.

"So the upshot is Courtney and I get $85,000 per annum until we marry?" Darcy questioned, her voice slightly raised. "Presumably someone suitable to *you two* as trustees, when that amount will be doubled?'

"No one is going to tell you who you can marry Darcy," Curt said carefully. "I'm sure everyone here will be hoping and praying you're not led into marrying the wrong man."

"Which is probably why I'll wait until forty to choose. There's no question sexual involvement lowers the I.Q. and since women don't have all that much anyway! We don't get the money outright."

"No." Adam shook his head. "Your father was adamant on that point."

"The capital will be required for the running of the station and your father's other affairs that were explained to you," Curt explained. "There's no upping the annual figure, I'm afraid. Your father's wishes stand. Personally I think it should be more given the size of the fortune but as trustee and executor I assure you neither of you will need for anything."

"I have grave misgivings about that!" Darcy found it obligatory to register a protest.

"How do *you* feel, Courtney?" Curt asked kindly. "We all know how Darcy feels."

"Shell shocked," she answered truthfully. "$85,000 annually is a fortune to me, I have no argument with that. But I feel strongly Darcy has been cheated out of her fair share. Can't we do something about that?"

Adam regarded her with his unfathomable eyes. "We can, Courtney," he said smoothly. "Darcy has a good case."

"So your tyranny never ends," said Darcy, staring up at her father's portrait. "I'm still shackled."

"Only if you persist in looking at it like that," Curt focused on her unhappy face, which he saw as yet another set-back in their stormy relationship.

"Did your dad shackle you?" Her beautiful eyes flashed. "You bet your life he didn't. You're the best son and heir a man could have. *You* have full authority over everything. There was no keeping you in chains. I can just imagine how you'd react, Curt, if you had to go to trustees cap in hand. No, you're the glorious male born to handle power."

"A *man* is the one thing you need, Darcy," Curt retorted, his own eyes sparking. "I understand your frustrations. Your father's will has complicated both our lives but I had no hand in making it. Neither did Adam. Our task was and remains carrying out your father's wishes."

"I want to do up the homestead," Courtney suddenly announced , sitting up straight and looking at her sister as though seeking her permission. "Not on a budget either."

"Surely you can't drop everything? You must have to return to your job?" Adam sounded very keen to know. He folded his arms across his chest, leaning back in the swivel chair.

Courtney shot him a haughty look. "I want you to know I'll decide that, thank you, Adam. With your permission, Darcy." She turned to her sister. "I'd like to stay on for a while. May I? I have extended leave."

Darcy let her head fall back helplessly. "Why ask me?" she said with wry humour. "You've just learned you get half of everything. For better or worse. That means

Murraree. If you want to do up the place go right ahead. It's okay by me. Whether it's okay by Curt is another nerve-racking story."

"Why don't we call it a night," said Curt rising to his impressive height. "What were you thinking of, Courtney? Calling in a decorator?"

"Sure," she said. "The house is desperately in need of renovation. I couldn't do it all myself."

"I realise that," Curt said. "Get some good design people out here. My mother might be able to help you with names. You and Darcy can get all your ideas together. Submit a plan. Costing I understand won't be exact."

"Am I hearing correctly?" Darcy asked, opening her eyes scornfully wide. "You're actively encouraging Courtney?"

"I am." He looked down at her, thinking Darcy always took the hard way around things." I'm assuming you're not going to go completely over the top?"

"Well I never!" Darcy spread her hands wide. "Just so we can be absolutely sure. We don't have to be stingy with this?"

"Not at all. The place is in need of restoration and modernizing. The money's there. I feel heartened you're going to take an interest, Darcy," Curt said with a decided lick of sarcasm. "That side of things hasn't been high in your education." He moved towards the door. "I'll say goodnight before you start to pick a fight. I want to get away fairly early in the morning. I *do* have a station to run forgive me for drawing your attention to the fact. I have to drop Adam off as well so he can hook up with his charter flight for Brisbane."

Courtney sat bolt upright. "You're leaving in the morning?" She met Adam's dark eyes.

He arched one black brow. "What's the matter? Will you miss me?"

"No!" she answered, fretting for hours afterwards.

* * *

Darcy spent a long time cooling off in the shower. Afterwards she pampered her body in a way she didn't do often, moisturizing then scenting her skin, brushing her long hair until it crackled. Later she padded around in her bedroom naked except for her satin nightgown, lemon in colour and decorated around the low V neck, down the sides and the split hemline with fine lace and embroidered roses. She had bought it on a mad impulse—she couldn't tear her eyes from it—on her last trip to Brisbane, over a year ago. She hadn't worn it thinking it too pretty but tonight she was feeling…too febrile…too sexy. She ached with it.

She always went too far with Curt, forever on the alert to question his authority when authority came off him in waves. He wouldn't come. He was fed up with her maddening behaviour. And who could blame him. She shifted to the verandah, enjoying the night breeze on her body. She could feel her skin's texture against the slinky satin. She gazed out over the moonlit expanse of the garden with its deeply shadowy pockets. The fronds of the palms were just barely moving. She had often felt she needed a huge space to breathe in, now she was starting to feel disconnected. As if with her father gone and Courtney eventually returning to her own world she would be left quite alone. She knew she was in danger of exhausting Curt's patience, constantly tormenting him with the fears and anxieties that had dominated her life and tied her in knots. It all had to stop. She couldn't keep dwelling on the past. She had to push into the future.

Curt had to know the truth before any of that could happen. She would have to find the courage to show him the photographs. When they had been revealed it might make the next part a little easier in the telling. The photographs were taken years ago but they were a big part of her sad story. What would he say? What would he *do* when she finished her sad recital? Would he pity her for what she had gone through or would he react with anger and disbelief? There was always that danger. There was so much at stake.

How could you have done this, Darcy. How could you have done this to yourself. To me?

That sort of reaction frightened her. Darcy dropped her face into her hands. No matter. Curt wasn't blameless. The photographs proved that.

She returned to the bedroom going to the Victorian cabinet-on-chest that held most of the things she felt that mattered. Things her mother had left behind. Little pieces of costume jewellery, silk scarves, lace edged handkerchiefs, half finished bottles of perfume, even make-up. There were the lovely little enamelled butterfly clips that once had nestled in Courtney's blonde curls…bright ribbons…her school awards—she'd forgotten she'd been such a bright student…riding trophies. In the bottom drawer of the chest tucked away in the manila folder they had come in, the photographs that had mortally wounded her and changed her life.

Why on earth hadn't she confronted Curt with them? She knew perfectly well why. But she could never speak of it. Even now she couldn't permit herself to curse her dead father for what he had done. He had been straight forward about it as was his way. He'd set out to prove Curt Berenger wasn't the heroic figure she thought he was. He was a man like other men with a man's appetites.

If I'd misjudged him Darcy I'd feel bad about it. But I haven't. Look at these! Don't turn and run. He's making a fool of you, girl!

Darcy shook the photographs out onto the bed. She ritually looked at them whenever she could bear it. There were four in all. Large black and white glossies. Two people were in all of them. Curt and a beautiful girl with a waterfall of long smooth dark hair. In one he was holding her aloft laughing up into her radiant face. In the second they were walking down a street together. He had his arm around her and she was staring up at him with a look of adoration no one could mistake. In the third they were having an al fresco coffee together. She had one hand stretched across the table to him while his whole body inclined towards her. Love showed in every line. The last photograph broke her heart. There was such emotion in it. Curt was hugging the girl to him while she laid her head trustingly against his heart.

You can bet your life, girl, they had sex together.

Why had she believed her father so totally? She'd been devoted to him certainly but Curt was the man she loved with all her heart. Curt was the fever in her blood.

He's flawed just like the rest of us and it's taken me, your father, to open your eyes.

Open her eyes. That was what her father had done. He didn't shy away from unpleasantness. By the time Curt had left for a trip to Brisbane, supposedly on business for his father McIvor had already arranged for a private investigator to follow his movements.

She'd said little at the time beyond a stricken, "How *could* you, Dad?"

It seems to me it's my duty, girl!

Several days later with Curt due home the following week she had suffered a miscarriage when it had never crossed her mind she was pregnant. No morning sickness, no nothing. No change in her breasts. Of course it was early days and missed periods weren't unusual for her with her strenuous life style.

She had handled it all on her own. The physical pain. The mental agony. Then when she was able, claiming she wasn't well—her appearance bore testament to that—she took the helicopter to the Koomera Crossing Bush Hospital where Doctor Sarah McQueen took charge of her. She would never forget Doctor Sarah's understanding and kindness. She had actually spent two days in hospital trying to heal an unhealable wound. She had told her father it was a rumbling appendix. He didn't care so long as she was back home.

"It was for the best, Darcy," Doctor McQueen had smiled at her with such sympathy and held her hand. "Nature's way of telling you. There's no reason whatever you can't have other children but next time, Darcy, you must remember to take it easy. No long strenuous hours in the saddle. You know that."

Curt came home to a very different Darcy. A changed woman. Nothing seemed important other than she had lost their baby. Lost their baby when the man she adored was running around with another woman. No, not a woman. Just a girl with a lovely coltish body. How it all started she didn't know but while she waited and shrank from the inevitable Curt didn't act on his big city romance. And all the while her father drove her crazy telling her she'd done the right thing.

Why if you married him you'd have to cope with his infidelities for the rest of your life.

Darcy slid the photographs she had lived with into the manila folder and shoved it to the back of the drawer. Even now they had the power to devastate her. She had fretted terribly in the days before her miscarriage, trying to lose herself in hard work. Of course she hadn't been aware she was pregnant so she needed no forgiveness nevertheless she *couldn't* forgive herself. She constantly thought about their child. How it would have looked had it lived. She envisaged a beautiful healthy child. She had no one outside Doctor Sarah to help her over it and she had to keep her inner devastation from her father. It had been a terrible time. How could it have been otherwise? She couldn't forgive herself. Curt mightn't forgive her either.

Her mind fled away to what she was going to do about the will. It wasn't the money. There was far more of it than she had ever imagined. Probably her frugal way of life had helped. In view of the tremendous amount of money her father had left, it seemed clear he'd been nothing short of a miser. The fact he had overlooked her contribution and unswerving loyalty was the really *killing* thing. It had pushed her to a new level of thought. She had expected to be highly suspicious of Courtney but her feelings of suspicion and hostility had been at most fleeting. All she could see was her little sister, the one she had loved and protected. Hating was a terrible way of life.

She was drawn back to the radiant beauty of the night. There was movement in the garden. Someone was out there watching her. Instantly she came out of her troubled reverie. She moved to the balustrade, staring towards the shadowy pockets of the garden. Her heart was thumping, not with fright—no one could hurt her here on her own land—but a wayward excitement so powerful it almost paralysed her.

She knew every inch of the extensive grounds, the massive date palms, the desert oaks, the low growing colonies of drought tolerant shrubs with their silver and sage foliage, the raised beds of perennials that smelled so sweetly, pervading the area with their unforgettable scents.

There near the giant panicles of bell flowers! She saw him clearly now. The outline of a tall, rangy man, the gleam of his pale shirt. He raised his hand in salute.

"Curt," she whispered, intent on tracking his progress.

He was making for the rear stairs which led to the side verandah and her bedroom. Courtney had her mother's old room which faced the front of the homestead. Adam was in the west wing where Curt was supposed to be. She had several rooms of the east wing to herself. Her own choice. Her own haven.

He was coming! It seemed like a miracle.

She heard a timber floorboard creak as she rushed down the verandah, her freshly shampooed hair a cloud of scented softness all around her. She felt flooded with adrenalin, a great surge of it, desire mixed with extreme nervousness. What was it he really wanted of her? A woman for all seasons? A wife, a mother for his children? Had he decided he really *needed* her? That's what it was all about. She *had* to be needed. She had never been needed in her whole life.

He was there at the top of the stairs before her, darkly handsome sculpted features, eyes shining, reaching for her with such purpose, such strength and hunger she felt faint.

"You didn't really think you were going to escape, did you?" he asked, low-voiced. His mouth moved down over her cheek to her throat, revelling in her woman's softness against his hard frame, the fragrance of her hair and her skin, her body naked beneath the seductive satin, begging to be touched. An avalanche of pleasure!

She knew from the look in his eyes and his lovely harsh breathing he was going to spend the night in her bed, the two of them going off into their own world, marvelling at its richness.

The time she had spent on herself had been done to please him. Now she felt incandescent. Desire for him danced in her head and her blood. She wasn't as naïve as she'd been in those long-ago days. She knew how to protect herself.

"I'm glad you're wearing that nightdress," he murmured so softly, she could barely hear him. "I'll let you keep it on for a little while."

Without another word he lifted her high in his arms, carrying her along the verandah to the moon drenched bedroom that was waiting for them.

She reached for him, but her hand clutched at air.

What time was it?

Darcy opened her eyes. Sunlight was flooding the room. Curt wasn't there, but every detail of his splendid body was imprinted on her flesh. She had fallen off to sleep with his arms encircling her, her body curled into his like a fern's frond. For as long as she lived she would never forget what had happened within these very walls. The magic of returning his loving without restraint.

Now she was shocked at how late it was. Eight-thirty. She had developed a ritual of waking at dawn. How Curt had managed to get himself up and away was proof of his vastly superior strength. She would have thought they had exhausted all their energy making love through the night. She was still basking in the wondrous after-effects. She stretched luxuriously like a cat beneath the sheet he must have thrown over her. She still felt abuzz. Her nightgown—a wicked indulgence that had paid off—was lying in a lustrous pool on the rug. Hadn't she subconsciously foreseen the night she would be wearing it? Curt had made her feel dazzlingly beautiful, womanly. He had melted her very skin.

For a fleeting second she considered staying in bed all day. Revelling in the sheer decadence. The past was the past. Mightn't it be preferable to let it lie? Make a fresh start? Doctor Sarah would never divulge her secret. Was that the way to handle it? Or was it wrong? There she was again, taking two steps forward and two steps back. But last night had been a triumph. No one could rob her of that.

She found Courtney in the kitchen, comforted by the sweet smile that hadn't an ounce of speculation in it.

"You look like you're floating," Courtney smiled. "The men have gone."

"Damn, I slept in." Darcy sat down at the kitchen table. "The first time since I can't remember when."

"It did you good," Courtney said with approval. "You look radiant. What would you like for breakfast? I've squeezed some orange juice. There's one of the Bowen mangoes left. They were lovely. Some scrambled eggs, maybe?"

Darcy gave her sister her first truly uncomplicated smile. "That would be a feast! Dad and I got into the way of having a light breakfast then taking off on the job. Not the way to do it, I know, but it was easier to placate him. One had to tread very carefully with Dad."

"You must have had a rotten time," Courtney said, pouring a glass of orange juice and placing it before her sister.

"Thanks." Darcy picked up the glass. "It's weird, but I never saw it then. Everything I did I did for love. It wasn't until you turned up and Dad bundled me into the background I got the message. I suppose if he hadn't died I could have gone on sacrificing my life. For a little while longer anyway. What time did they leave?"

"Well before seven. Curt was anxious to get away." She shook off thoughts of Adam and the way he had looked at her before he left. Dark eyes on hers the whole time. Challenging, knowing, mocking. *Intimate.* As though they had crossed some boundary together. It shook her, stripping her of her customary poise. She had never seen such a look in another man's eyes. "Curt has some stock agent coming," she added belatedly. "Ted something..." Courtney searched her memory bank for the name, but the only name that stuck was *Adam.*

"Jensen," Darcy supplied, downing her orange juice, cold and delicious.

"That's it!" Courtney began to whip up the eggs and cream.

"Did you fix them breakfast like me?" Darcy smiled.

"I did. Curt's so easy to be around, but I can't say the same for Adam. He really puts me on the defensive."

"He's a lawyer, dear." Darcy smiled. "By the way, I'm not going to contest the will."

Courtney gazed back, almost desperately. "It wasn't fair. We all know it wasn't. I don't need all that money, Darcy. I'd probably be happier without it."

"Nevertheless we'll share it," Darcy said, with genuine acceptance. "The one thing I don't want you doing is interfering in the affairs of the station. You simply don't know anything about it."

Courtney's expression was rueful. She set the mixing bowl down on the table. "But I want to, Darcy. Surely you can appreciate that? It's my heritage too, but I promise I'll defer to your judgment. As far as I'm concerned, you're the Boss."

"You mean Curt's the Boss," Darcy answered wryly, a little taken aback by her sister's fervour. "I'm absolutely certain Adam will have his say as well. Let's face it, he's the legal eagle."

"And doesn't he act it," Courtney said, with uncharacteristic waspishness. "But obviously we need one." She resumed what she was doing. "I just hate it the way he looks at me." Her smooth cheeks turned pink. "It spooks me." *And excites.* "I don't see trust there."

"Lawyers are like that. Suspicious," Darcy soothed, enjoying the delicious flavour of the mango. "So you want to be part of the action?"

"I certainly do. I'll do my very best to learn."

"There's a lot you can learn," Darcy said, feeling a sense of pleasure in her sister. "I'm all for female empowerment, but running a station this size needs a man. It's just too tough. A farm we could handle. A big cattle station, no. You've met Dad's overseer, Tom McLaren. He's a good man. Dad depended on him a lot but Tom wouldn't want full responsibility for running the station. He took orders. Like me. Dad was like a battle ship, and we all followed in his wake. Then there are his other business affairs. He was masterly at business if not as a husband and father. It's going to be a big job."

"I'm well aware of that," Courtney said, turning over the situation in her mind.

"But we've got help," Darcy said briskly. "McIvor brought in the top guns, which isn't to say they're going to run everything their way, damn it. That I'm not prepared to take lying down."

"I see no reason why we should. I do think Dad put a lot on Curt, knowing what a big job he has already."

"He's up to it," Darcy said. "My impression of Adam is he's a straight shooter. I can't see him acting unethically in any circumstances. Curt went into bat for him. Dad was antagonistic towards Adam probably because Adam wasn't in awe of him. Dad expected that and mostly he got it. Dad liked people to cringe a little."

"Even I remember that." Courtney turned away to the refrigerator for some butter. "Are you sure you're okay with my doing up the homestead?"

"Good grief, yes. It desperately needs doing up. I wasn't able to do much. Dad always said he couldn't tolerate change. What he really couldn't tolerate was handing over money. It's not uncommon with rich men."

"Mum must have had the right people working for her to have managed such a good divorce settlement," Courtney said wryly.

"And how he hated it! I used to think I would *never* marry hearing Dad rave on about infidelity and divorce. Come to that I'm not married."

"You will be," Courtney said as though nothing on earth could prevent it.

Darcy could feel herself flush. To cover it she made a business of tucking a long strand of hair back. "Though I'm tempted to laze about all day, I thought when we're finished here, we might step into Dad's study. I seldom got invited in. I used to do a lot of accounting work for him in the evening but in my own study. There was lots of stuff he wouldn't let me in on. I wouldn't be surprised if all his chickens came home to roost one day and we'll have to sort it out. Know much about book keeping?"

"I have a degree in Business Administration," Courtney said modestly, pouring the egg mixture into the pan.

"Gosh, what a master stroke!" Darcy burst out laughing.

"I'm absolutely certain I can help you," Courtney waited patiently for the eggs to set before she began stirring.

"What about your own job?" Darcy asked after a minute. "You must enjoy it?" She realized with a decided pang she would miss Courtney dreadfully when she went away. Only so much a girl should be expected to bear.

Courtney removed the eggs from the heat, then ladled them onto a warm plate.

"You make me want to start thumbing through cook books." Darcy looked at the creamy pile with approval. "So what about the job?"

Courtney sat down at the huge kitchen table. "I enjoy it of course, but I want you to know." Her voice broke a little. "I don't enjoy anything as much as being here with you."

Darcy was quiet for a moment, fighting the old demons that weren't ready to give in. "That's lovely, Courtney, but is it the truth?" She had to protect herself against future shocks.

For answer, Courtney reached out and seized hold of her sister's hand. "Yes, it *is* the truth. Don't *you* start seeing me as someone you can't trust. For all the years we've been apart I would have thought you'd know the essential me better than that?"

"But you'll go away." Darcy's jewel coloured eyes looked into the middle distance. "You'll get a kick out of doing up the house—I will too—then your old, glamorous life will beckon."

"What glamorous life?" Courtney scoffed. "It's a nice life, sure, but I definitely want more than I'm getting. I want my sister back. I want my family back. I want to work on something that's my own. I never left Murraree because I wanted to, Darcy. I left because I was forced to go with Mum. I love Murraree too. I'm damned sure I can learn to ride a horse."

"Of course you can," Darcy harrumphed. "Dad perfected the art of frightening the hell out of you. What are you trying to say?"

"What I'm trying to say." Courtney leaned across the table,

her big blue eyes earnest. "I'd like to stay. We always were terrifically compatible. You remember that don't you?"

"You were the sweetest little thing," Darcy said gently. She remembered all the nights after they'd gone when she eventually fell off to sleep with her pillow wet with tears.

Courtney said nothing for a moment, overcome. "So I can help you, Darcy. You need help. Together we can achieve a lot more than if we stood alone. I love you. You're very special to me."

So eager to please! Darcy found it nigh impossible to keep her distance. When she looked up, the light of fire was in her eyes. "For one thing, we could show the men the calibre of the women they're dealing with," she said decisively.

"Show them our true worth," Courtney seconded.

"Even Dad said I was as sharp as a tack," Darcy reminisced. "You know, I think I've got goose bumps." She rubbed her hands up and down her bare arms.

"I have too," Courtney laughed. "If it suits you, I'd love to make Murraree my home. We'd be together. I'd have to go back to Brisbane to finalise my affairs but I'd be back as soon as I could. There are plenty standing in line for my job so my boss wouldn't be too upset. You shouldn't be here alone, anyway."

Darcy felt it necessary to issue the warning. "It's not an easy life, Courtney," she said, looking at her sister hard. "Don't burn all your bridges. It would break my heart to see you wilt out here. Mum did." It was the first time she had been able to manage that one precious word. *Mum.*

"Yes, she did, but I'm not our mother. I'm a stronger person, Darcy. Like you I didn't break under the deprivation we both suffered. I'm a serious woman with serious ideas. Murraree is our inheritance. Let's make it work."

CHAPTER NINE

AND make it work they did. As a *team* Darcy discovered with her sister taking over the domestic duties and most of the paper work she was freed up to supervise the on going work on the station. Without really waiting for Curt's approval—she certainly made sure she told him—she had hired another couple of station hands and taken on a jackeroo, an adventurous young man who wanted an action packed year on an Outback station before taking up his University studies. All three new employees were settling in quickly enough though Tom McLaren, a highly proficient bushman, had to keep an eye on the new jackeroo who had more than a touch of derring-do for his own good.

The excitement of restoration was well underway. It had began the same week Courtney had returned from cutting her ties in Brisbane. Hugh De Lisle, a designer who had begun his career as an architect, and who had masterminded restorations for several well-known pastoral families had taken on the job. It was Kath Berenger who had acted as go-between having availed herself of De Lisle's services some years before.

He and his assistant Harriet Gibson had arrived by charter flight. De Lisle, in his late forties, came across as a charming affable man who understood how to get on with clients, listened to their likes and dislikes, allowed them input at the same time knowing exactly what he intended to do. Harriet, an elegant Madonna-like creature had surprisingly little to say, leaving it to her boss but obviously she too knew what she was about.

Darcy was shown everything, samples of this and that, colour charts, beautiful swatches for draperies and sofas, so many she was dizzy. The major rooms were to be tackled first. Hugh with his all-seeing creative eyes took in the crumbling beauty, the genteel shabbiness and the mad jostling of paintings and furniture without comment. Darcy expected he would be dismayed with what he saw, but to her surprise he expressed the opinion they were really going to like the homestead when he had finished.

"You have so many marvellous things!" Harriet was heard to murmur.

"We'll need painters, plasterers, plumbers, and I would suggest you might like to think of hiring a good landscape designer to begin certain clearing and restoration of the home gardens which could look magnificent," Hugh said, not seriously expecting they would disagree. "I know an excellent design company should you decide to include the garden as well. I think you should."

"And spend more money?" Darcy whispered to her sister as they walked out onto the verandah that morning. Darcy was rapidly coming to the realisation she had grown up with Scrooge.

"Curt gave us a free hand." Courtney reminded her, accompanying Darcy to the station jeep. "I know you're a bit apprehensive but nothing has been done for years and years. Look at it this way, it's not as though money is tight. Father left a fortune. He might have set a limit to our personal spending but that's not going to stop us from bringing the homestead back to life. Did you know there are some wonderful chandeliers in the attic? Big antique mirrors, Persian rugs all rolled up with mothballs. Furniture."

"Goodness, I thought we had enough." Darcy commented wryly.

Courtney's face was full of light. It was obvious she was having a lot of fun. "We'll only use the best. Hugh wants to bring back the homestead's soul. He's a sensitive man. He must have felt the house had lost it. And oh, the ideas when it's time to get around to the kitchen!" She stood there smiling up into her sister's face.

"I'm so glad *you're* here, Courtney," Darcy said, feeling she would never have the time to oversee such an operation. "I can see you're getting a thrill out of it. So am I. Don't think I'm not. It's very pleasant and informative to listen to creative people talk, but I have to keep doing my job which is taking care of the station."

"So what's on the agenda today?" Courtney asked.

"A burn off," Darcy said, staring up at the brilliantly enamelled blue sky. "Murraree carries huge areas of spinifex. Tom and I have picked out some areas for the burn. The cattle love the spinifex short and green so the place will benefit from a selective burn."

"You've got men to control it?"

"Of course." Darcy nodded calmly. "The big muster in another month. All the clean skins have to be brought in. They like to hide away in the swamps." She nibbled her bottom lip. "I have to talk to Curt about replacing the Bell helicopter. It's had its day. We want the muster all over by Christmas."

"Most of the work on the house will be finished by then," Courtney said, her blue eyes kindling with excitement. "Have you time to fit in another riding lesson this afternoon, or too busy?"

"I'll make it," Darcy tipped her akubra further over her eyes. "You should be very happy with your progress. You've done the groundwork. I know Zack usually has the horses ready and waiting but I feel tacking up is all part of the learning process."

"And it's fun," Courtney said. "Every lesson is fun. It was the exact opposite with Father. I'll never to able to ride like you though. You look marvellous in the saddle."

"It takes time to achieve excellence. I've had enough practice," Darcy said, but in truth she was a natural with an in-built love and understanding of horses. "By the way," Darcy turned back. "There are excellent carpenters and jack of all trades on the station to help out. I'll round them up and send them up to the house. Hugh can speak to them. See if they can handle what's required."

"Great!" Courtney gave a delighted little laugh. "We'll have plenty to report to the men when they show up."

"Curt will be a week or two in the Territory," Darcy reminded her. "He's pretty heavily involved in a take-over."

"But he'll be back." Courtney waved happily. "And won't he see some changes! That superior being, Adam, too. I can't wait to surprise him."

Over the following six weeks workmen swarmed all over the ground floor of the homestead. Painters. Plasterers. Carpenters. Electricians. The two magnificent matching chandeliers went up in the drawing room. A little harassed after the *quietness* of her life Darcy found herself tripping over drop sheets. They lay everywhere. There were constant loud noises what with workmen calling to one another, machines in operation, ladders being shifted, and clanging buckets. Darcy found she was quite pleased to go off on her rounds and leave her sister to it.

It worked extremely well that Courtney was the domesticated one. She thrived on it. She liked to talk to the workmen, very pleasantly as Darcy always noticed, but still ensuring she got the best out of them. Courtney was a great communicator which was probably why she'd won her former job. Now and again Darcy asked her if she missed it, but the answer was always a resounding, no!

Harriet, a little more talkative without her boss, had returned with all the new drapes. They were hung in the drawing room, the formal dining room and at the French doors of the adjoining library. Without question, they instantly transformed each room. This was before the new custom made sofas arrived and the furniture was rearranged. Many pieces were ruthlessly dispatched to the attic while other pieces were brought down.

When Curt arrived back on Sunset from the Territory he only took a day to fly over to check out progress. "Well I'll be damned!" He stood staring around the drawing room, clearly impressed. "What a transformation! My mother just has to see this."

"She will, she will!" Darcy promised while Courtney stood there smiling to herself.

The elegant Harriet who thus far hadn't given the impression of much joie de vivre, now surprised the sisters with a dramatic sea change. She trailed Curt wherever he went, her face tilted to his, eager and expectant, savouring all his comments as if they were meant only for her.

"I think she's met her perfect man," Courtney whispered to Darcy behind her hand.

"If she keeps it up I think I'll throw something at her," Darcy returned, half amused, half outraged, by Harriet's flirtatious manner with *her* man. "I don't know whether you realize it but it seems Hugh—never mind us—had very little input." Harriet now had hold of Curt's arm steering him through to the library.

"Can you believe this woman?" Courtney was reduced to the giggles. "She's hardly had two words to say to us, but she's all over Curt. I suggest we get in there."

Darcy only nodded, wondering if any woman could keep a man like Curt entirely to herself.

Later on she and Curt took the jeep down to one of the yards where Charlie Big Hawk, the best of the aboriginal stockmen was breaking in the pick of the brumbies. Horses are not inherently rideable. Horse breaking is a highly skilled task involving mouthing, riding and educating. When they arrived at the yard Charlie was transmitting instructions in a soft melodious voice to a fine looking chestnut. "Slow down, stop, turn left, turn right, back up." It was all done via the reins to the bit in the mouth.

"There's one out of a station mare that got away," Curt said instantly.

"I can tell you which mare," Darcy said. "It was Lady Luck. She never did come back."

"It's behaving well for a wild horse." Curt narrowed his eyes against the dust and glare.

"Charlie has streamlined his job. He's a master. And no you can't have him. Charlie always hands over well mouthed horses that can be easily handled. We've both seen plenty of wild horses who won't let anyone get near them."

Curt nodded absently. "The rogues. Bite, rear, strike out savagely. Every station has had occasional serious injury. Terrified horses wild or not are very dangerous creatures. How's Courtney going with the riding lessons?" He turned to face her. She looked beautiful, aglow with health and nowhere near as vulnerable as she had been with McIvor around.

"She's doing quite well," Darcy said, smiling. "She sits correctly. She's got good balance and she's mastered all the basic aids. The great thing is she's getting pleasure out of it and I'm getting pleasure out of seeing how well she's doing."

"So you've bonded?" Curt asked gently.

She raised her head and looked at him. "Marvellously well. She is my sister after all. At first I was determined to keep my distance, but it didn't work out that way."

"Because you're a generous person," Curt said. "I know there are lots of things going on in your life at the moment, but what about us?" She could see the powerful feeling in his green eyes.

"You won't believe how I've missed you," she said.

"So what are we going to do about it?" He lifted a farewell hand to Charlie then drew Darcy away to the shade of the trees. "I need you, Darcy. I've waited long enough. When I lost you I thought there was something that had gone bitterly wrong. You've as good as admitted that yourself. I know your father was somehow to blame but even a father shouldn't be able to come between a man and woman in love."

"He's gone now, Curt," she said the old feelings of guilt and grief abruptly rolling over her.

"I wish you could talk about it."

She looked back at him helplessly. "I just can't." Her mind veered away from direct confrontation. Not now when things were going so well.

"All right," he sighed. "I don't know what your father could ever have said or done for you to change your mind about me."

"It's over, Curt. That part of my life is over."

"My poor sweet Darcy!" He lifted her hand and kissed it. "Just as well I want you so desperately."

She looked up at him gravely, her aquamarine eyes blazing in the gold of her face. "You want to marry me?"

"Don't you agree with marriage?" he asked with a twisted smile. "I don't want you for my mistress, Darcy. I want us to be together always. I want you to be the mother of my children."

That shook her badly. The emotional tears welled into her eyes. If she could have changed anything in the world it would have been not to have lost their child. "If only we could go back in time," she grieved.

He stared at her, a puzzled man for a very long time. "You talk in riddles, Darcy. I've never learned that skill. It troubles me there's so much left unspoken. Sometimes I think I can't endure it. All I know is, one day things were perfect for us. I remember I had to take a trip to Brisbane for Dad. When I came back you were in one hell of a state. You told me you didn't want to see me any more. My sense of emptiness was profound. Can't you understand that? Didn't you owe me some kind of explanation."

Vivid rose stained her skin. "I promised you. One day I'd tell you the full story."

"And I have to be content with that?" he asked in utter frustration.

"I'm begging you," she said, feeling too heavily at peril.

He stared at her, his handsome face suddenly losing colour. "I couldn't have got you pregnant, could I? No, of course not." He shook his head, half closing his eyes at the very idea. "You would have told me."

It was her moment, but at the sheer disbelief in his expression, she lost her nerve. "Yes," she said, when she meant: *Yes, I should have told you.*

"Don't make it another long wait, Darcy," he warned. "I'm tired of waiting." He shifted his hands to her shoulders. "Do you love me or do you only love me when you're locked in my arms?"

She turned ardent eyes on him. "I've always loved you, Curt. There's never been anyone else for me." She stared up at him intently. "Are you sure there hasn't been someone for you?" Someone with a waterfall of smooth dark hair and a delicate coltish body.

He answered quite matter-of-factly. "I've had my affairs, Darcy," he said not shifting his gaze. "You know that. It was only because I couldn't get any love out of you. For that matter you allowed a couple of guys to come courting."

"Maybe, but it was always you," she said softly. "Always you." She didn't care who was watching. She wrapped her arms around him.

"That's good, because you'll never be free of me," Curt vowed. "What if we announce our engagement at Christmas? That will give everyone a little time to figure out their plans. You'll want to tell Courtney though I don't think she'll be in the least surprised. Married before June because I have to tell you I can't hold out any longer."

It was a struggle to recover her breath. It was pretty miraculous to have a second chance. "But Christmas is almost upon us," she laughed.

"All the better. I need to get a brand on you, don't I?" he purred. "My woman."

"Darcy Berenger." It wasn't the first time she'd tried that name out on her tongue. "Dad knew this was going to happen." The irony of it when he had laboured to keep them apart.

"I'd say he was banking on it." Curt had an edge to his voice. "I wasn't to have you when he was alive, but he was perfectly agreeable to my having you after he was gone. By the way I've never been able to keep secrets from my mother. She's always known how I feel about you. Once I'm married she wants to go and live with Aunt Patricia. They want to travel. Mum has a big itinerary lined up and so has Pat. She has a very clever granddaughter living in New York. Pat adores her."

"But what of Courtney?" Darcy suddenly came down to earth. She wouldn't be unable to live happily ever after if Courtney were left on her own. "I've only just found her. I can't let her go."

"Of course not," Curt tutted. "I don't want you to let her go either. But she can't come on our honeymoon. Besides, I don't think Courtney will be on her own long," he added, a smile in his voice.

"Do you know something I don't know?" Darcy searched his face.

"She and Adam have something going haven't they?" he asked, with a lift of one brow.

"Adam? Are you mad? She doesn't even like him."

"Oh really?" Curt put his arm around her shoulder, feeling a near primitive sense of possession. He led her back to the jeep. "It seemed to me there's a lot of unfinished business there. I could be wrong. We'll see. I've already invited him for the polo weekend. You and Courtney are staying over, of course. We're the hosts."

"That'll be lovely," Darcy breathed, her emotions running at full throttle.

He looked down at her, "What do you say we go somewhere where I can kiss you senseless."

She coloured and touched his cheek. "That sounds wonderful. What about Crystal Creek?"

"Perfect!" His voice had the deep seductive tones of a lover.

The polo crowd was out in force. Many had been invited to the gala ball in Sunset's Great Hall, others had come from near and far to watch the fastest game in the world and enjoy the lavish nonstop refreshments. Kath Berenger was a marvellous hostess— It was something at which she'd had plenty of practice so the day went wonderfully well.

Unlike tennis where no novice would ever be paired with a champion, polo was different. Teams were generally matched according to the aggregate handicap of individuals so newcomers to the game often found themselves competing with seasoned performers like Curt, a very colourful player indeed and several of his friends, scions of the various stations.

So it came to happen Curt's team against every probability *lost*. If he was disappointed—Curt liked to win—he didn't show the least bit of rancour and was notably kind to the lanky six-foot-three novice who would one day develop into an excellent player.

"Don't they look gorgeous! Absolutely superb!" A showy young brunette with a cheeky short haircut gushed. Barbra Vaughn had attached herself to the McIvor party although she'd been invited by Lara Rankin of neighbouring Cobalt Downs.

To her great surprise, if not pleasure—they had not been friends—Courtney had met up with Barbra outside one of the marquees. Barbra had lost out to Courtney for the public relations job and been pretty spiteful about it afterwards. As chance would have it Barbra had been invited out for the long week-end by Lara. It appeared they had gone to boarding school together. Courtney was sure it was Barbra who kept up the friendship. Barbra had been quite a name dropper. Courtney remembered she had once remarked when all the girls were out to lunch she only wanted to know people who were "on the up and up." The Rankins were a well known family in the Channel Country.

Barbra remained with them for quite a while playing up to Adam who was looking like some exclusive ad for men's designer clothes, expressing surprise and delight he was going to be at the ball. Barbra was too.

"You've made a conquest there," Courtney told him afterwards, watching her sister go up to Curt and kiss him on the cheek. She was feeling keenly it wouldn't be all that much longer before Darcy and Curt decided they couldn't remain apart. So where did that leave her? The sheer strangeness of life hit her. She had only found her sister to lose her. But no matter what she was going to stay on Murraree. It was her home. She was praying Darcy might eventually come around to allowing their mother to visit.

"What's the matter?" Adam asked, a questioning lift to his brow. The sun shining through the trees turned Courtney's hair to spun gold. She was wearing a luminous yellow outfit that looked perfect on her. A sleeveless top with a low round neck, the bodice adorned with little bows down the front, the skirt gently flowing. There couldn't have been a more feminine woman. Was she aware of the picture she made, so exquisitely beautiful people automatically smiled when they looked at her. Aware of it and clever enough to exploit it?

"Why nothing," she evaded, unwilling to share her thoughts with this enigmatic man.

"Obviously there is."

She sighed. "Okay, I was just thinking Curt won't want to share Darcy with me. They're in love."

"I don't think there's any doubt about that," Adam answered dryly. "But it won't take you long to find someone of your own, Courtney. Marriage isn't going to break up you sisters. Nothing will any more. The emotional attachment is too strong. The homestead looks marvellous. Darcy told me how much of that is due to you. She also told me how much she found herself relying on you."

"I have lots of hidden talents, Adam," she said, conscious there was always a feeling of sustained tension between them.

"Just sitting here looking at you, a great many of them are on show. Your looks, your smile, your charm. You captivate people. That's an enormous talent. You're a wonderfully pretty woman, Courtney McIvor." He held her gaze until she blinked and looked away.

"Thank you." Long used to hearing she was pretty Courtney flushed under his intense scrutiny. She might have been a butterfly under the microscope. "I can't take credit for it any more than Darcy can for her *real* beauty and her extraordinary eyes. It's in the genes. She won't hear of meeting our mother. When I begin to approach the subject she waves her hand as if to say, that's final!"

"I don't think final means final with Darcy," Adam said, a slight edge creeping into his voice. "She's nothing if not a loving, forgiving woman."

"So why do I think that's another crack at me?" Why couldn't he trust her? Was there something more in his own background to account for it? A blighted romance? He must have had many. Perhaps he had an aversion to pocket-sized blondes?

"You might be looking for more than is intended," he was

saying smoothly. "I'm going to ask you now while the going's good. If I wait until tonight I'll miss out entirely. Would you grant me the first and the last dance?"

She glanced away into the brilliant glare of the day, the players, the floats, the strings of polo ponies, the groups of people seated around the field, talking and laughing, the colourful array of bunting. Some young couples were lazing on the grass, obviously flirting and enjoying it immensely. The huge white marquees, offered food and drink. Guests swarmed around the entrances. "What have you done to deserve it?" she asked quietly, her body relaxed, her heart fluttering inside.

He smiled as though he recognized his own smile's persuasive powers. "I thought you'd be pleased as your lawyer and trustee funding for the restoration was approved without delay and without coming to blows."

"And we're not finished," she said, giving him a sideways glance. "I just thought I'd tell you. Next year we intend to start on upstairs. With the exception of my mother's room all the bedrooms and bathrooms need refurbishing. No point in having a marvellous old homestead if you can't invite lots of guests."

"So you see yourself staying?"

"Why sound so surprised?" she asked with quick challenge. "I was born here. Murraree is my home. I'm a lot tougher than I look."

He couldn't help it. He laughed. "Actually you look like the summer breeze could blow you away."

"There you go again!" she said crossly. "Even Darcy is waiting for me to wilt. But I won't. I was happy enough in the city but cities are man made buildings, however splendid. In the city all you have to relate to is buildings and people. Out here, there's the grandeur of nature to relate to. A world without horizons. The vast space. The exhilarating sense of freedom. The endless skies. The billions of big beautiful stars that come out at night." She shook her head. "You simply don't see stars like that in the cities. You don't see the larkspur ranges either, or the fantastic colour changes, the magical play of light, parallel lines of fiery sandhills curling at the top like waves. I can't wait to see the country after rain. As a little girl I used to glory in the wildflowers, the miles and miles of white and yellow bachelor buttons. Darcy and I used to make garlands for us to wear. Mum and the two of us. We were so close, in our world of flowers. I can still smell their scent on my skin."

He felt like he was breathing it in. "You're like a flower yourself." He was shocked by the sudden desire he felt. Shocked by its strength and its depth. She had spoken without artifice, such a shining light in her eyes he experienced a tingling right through his body. But flowerlike or not she was dangerous. A woman like that could get right under a man's skin. He rose from his planter's chair to free himself of her spell. "Wouldn't you like a cold drink?" He held out his hand to her enclosing its small softness.

"Yes I would." At the touch of skin on skin her eyelashes fell quivering onto her petalled cheeks.

"You haven't answered me by the way?" His lean features were taut with the effort of subduing his feelings. He didn't want her to see his emotions. It was like being stripped of his armour. He had been left powerless after his father had been taken so horribly from him. Being in control was important. "First and last dance?" And as many as I can possibly get in between. It was so easy to go forward. So difficult to backtrack. Something inexorable was impelling him towards this lovely, seemingly innocent young woman. Something that could change his ordered life.

She fell into step beside him not even reaching his shoulder. For a moment she had the strangest fancy they were cut off from the world. Just the two of them. "If you insist."

His eyes rested on her curls that licked up like golden flames around her face. "I do, even when I know you'd love to turn me down."

CHAPTER TEN

BY TEN o'clock the ball was in full swing.

Locked in Curt's arms Darcy felt such a current of sexual energy she thought the heat of it must be showing on her face.

Curt pulled her in close. "I love you," he mouthed near her ear thinking of the electrifying lovemaking that was coming his way. He had to have her. For years he had lived with nothing but memories that wouldn't go away. After all the music, the dancing, the lavish supper was over he was going to take her away with only the blossoming stars to light their way.

She looked so beautiful he felt he moved in her radiance. She had insisted Courtney was responsible for the way she looked: "Courtney dressed me up!" but her beauty was her own. He felt he was absorbing it as if through the very pores of his skin. Her dress was sheer magic. So romantic. He loved it. It hung from tiny straps, showing her beautiful breasts in a way she had never dared before, the material unbelievably the exact aquamarine as her eyes, embellished with sequins, diamantes, little crystals that sparkled in the lights. The dress was soft and floaty, chiffon, organza he didn't know but it caressed every inch of her willowy body then floated free to the floor.

She looked perfect. His woman. He had noted with pride how their entrance had made everyone sit up and take notice.

Darcy looked fabulous. It was a picture of her he would always carry in his head.

Across the huge hall Courtney surrendered her hand into Adam Maynard's with a leap of panic. Being in his arms was having a powerful effect on her. She could feel her insides contracting with an excitement she didn't really want. Even when they let go of each other in a dance movement he still felt overpoweringly close. She was a good dancer with natural rhythm. She had enjoyed her fair share of clubbing and great partners. She had somehow thought as he was so much the clever, self-contained lawyer, he might be—not self-conscious—he was too assured for that, but not able to match her on his feet.

She was wrong. So stupid. How could he possibly have two left feet with that elegant, graceful body though he didn't unwind with her like he did with that man eater, Barbra, who appeared to have gone wild over him. Barbra's dress was really bare on top, with a short skirt, cinched around the waist so the folds of the skirt were hiked up above the knees. She had great legs and she was showing a lot of skin. Actually she looked great, very sexy and raring for a good time. Barbra had looked over several times with a brilliant provocative smile for Adam but giving Courtney a look of barely concealed insolence. See what a washout you are beside me!

If Courtney was on her guard, she had reason to be. Barbra had taken a tremendous fancy to the handsome, inscrutable Adam. Man of mystery. She had already checked him out. A girl had to so as not to waste time. Word was he was a top lawyer with a prestigious firm; that he was in fact one of the trustees of the late Jock McIvor's estate. McIvor, it appeared had been a multimillionaire so the two sisters were heiresses. Sweet little Courtney with the perfect petite body in her oh so dreamy dress wasn't going to push her out of the action again. The extraordinary thing was no one had known about

Courtney's rich father. They had all assumed her parents had long since gone their separate ways.

Now this! Agog Barbra had discussed the whole situation with Lara, not that it had been easy. Lara had been loathe to entertain her friend with details of the McIvor girls' lives, but she had opened up a little as Barbra feigned genuine caring. After all, she and Courtney had been colleagues. Such a small world! So Lara had talked and Barbra had listened.

Out in the star-spangled night, with the Southern Cross glittering over their heads, Adam and Courtney were taking a breather. Other young couples were milling around the open doorways so they moved a little way off into the velvety darkness.

It was like taking a walk with a tiger. Courtney felt incredibly nervous. She had to keep reminding herself that this was out of character for her. She had certain rules and her boyfriends had to abide by them. She liked to think she played it cool, but the old techniques weren't working on Adam. Of course he was older, more experienced, more sophisticated. A man like that could hurt her. Damn it he was hurting her already.

Adam recognised she was wary of him. It was not surprising. He was wary of her. Yet she stood there a vision in her vertiginous high heeled gold sandals that gave her a few extra inches. Her dress with its intricate petalled skirt fell just short of her delicate ankles. It was a subtle tone of lemon with sequinned flashes of gold, turquoise and silver. She had beautiful taste for one so young, in her dressing and in her contribution to the refurbishing of Murraree homestead. "You're as jumpy as a kitten," he remarked.

There seemed to be a buzzing in Courtney's ears. "Maybe I'm too aware of you as a man," she heard herself saying.

"And you don't know how to handle it?" She could see his smile in the darkness. "That's hard to believe."

"I was just thinking the same myself," she admitted wryly. "Normally I love a challenge, but every nerve in my body warns me to steer clear of you, Adam."

He moved her a little further off, towards the shrubbery, his hand at her elbow. "If you're so full of wisdom, why have you allowed yourself to dance with me all night?"

"You mean when you haven't been dancing with Barbra?" she countered.

"Now there's someone who's jealous of you."

Courtney fingered the chiffon of her skirt. "Perhaps she's gained the wrong impression and thinks I'm with *you.*"

"Aren't you?" He gave a very attractive, very masculine laugh.

It made her whole body flame. She wasn't accustomed to men who were so sure of themselves. "I think I'll go back inside," she said, unconsciously tilting her chin.

"Wait a minute. Please." His fingers lightly encircled her wrist. "A lot of people seem to be having fun." They were in fact kissing. Some were even romping over the grass like puppies.

"Not *us!*" she cried in alarm, grateful the dark would hide her blush.

"Why not?" His voice made her heart flutter. "It seems to me I've wanted to since the first moment I laid eyes on you."

There could be no misunderstanding now. "Don't you dare!" Where oh where was her customary poise? "We shouldn't be out here."

But there was simply no stopping him. Her protest was cut off as he covered her mouth with his own. The expertise was fantastic. She felt at once profoundly helpless and incredibly desired. Something she had never expected. She had expected arrogance, being mastered. Instead he kissed her in a way that totally belied his mistrustful attitude towards her. She had been kissed many times before but it was never anything like this. He kissed her as though her mouth was some heavenly fruit he had long hungered after and now it was on offer.

It was too arousing. She broke away, her eyes huge in her pale face. "That was simply *over the top,* Adam," she seethed. "I hated it, nearly as much as I hate you."

He had the audacity to laugh. "I can't pretend I'm sorry, Courtney. Really I can't. I'll probably fantasise about it for the rest of my days."

He was mocking her. Of course he was. She could feel him staring after her.

Adam waited perhaps ten minutes after Courtney had stormed off. She was amazingly frisky on those high heels, he thought with amused admiration. He was on the alert to go after her in case she stumbled, but she didn't. He returned to the hall, hoping Barbra whatever her name was wasn't going to suddenly materialize out of the crowd and make a bee-line for him. He knew Barbra's type.

Instead he saw Barbra in *avid* conversation with Darcy. Darcy, very slender and beautiful as a goddess, had her dark head bent. She didn't look happy. In fact Darcy looked perturbed. Adam looked around quickly for Curt; saw him hemmed in by a group of polo fanatics. Adam moved towards Darcy, intending to get her away from this Barbra by asking her to dance.

She turned, her expression softening when she saw who it was. "Oh, Adam!" There was relief in her voice.

"My dance, I think." He smiled.

"Excuse us, won't you?" Darcy nodded regally to the now bug-eyed Barbra.

"What was that all about? You look upset." Adam ventured when they were out among the other dancers.

"I'm afraid I am," she admitted. "I was having a wonderful time too. I don't know that girl. I know she worked with

Courtney, but she literally clapped me on the back and began to tell me how clever Courtney is."

"Well isn't she?" Adam said, his voice dead calm, waiting for what was to come.

"Absolutely. Courtney has established that. But this Barbra started to tell me stories from the office. How Courtney had told them all about her multimillionaire father. How he wanted to see her after many years and how—just like the movies—he was dying. She told them he owned a famous cattle station with a heritage listed homestead and that she had an older sister. Me. She said her father had acted for years as though she never existed but she was going to wrap him around her little finger. 'We all knew she could! Courtney is the ultimate charmer and boy does she make good use of it!' was what she said. Courtney has quite a reputation according to Barbra."

"I think we can safely label Barbra a bitch?" Adam commented impassively.

Darcy's eyes flashed. "I felt like pushing her aside and telling her to get lost. She told me how quickly Courtney had gone up the ladder. What she'd been prepared to do to make it. She's ruined my night. How could she talk that way about Courtney?"

"Pure jealousy," Adam said, his voice grim.

"Courtney wouldn't have talked like that," Darcy said loyally. "It's not her. Yet how did this Barbra come to know so much?"

"She probably coaxed it out of the friend she's staying with," Adam suggested.

Darcy shook her head emphatically. "Not Lara. Lara is a very nice person. I've known her since forever. I can't see Lara indulging in malicious gossip. The worst thing is, I'm suddenly reminded we were all suspicious of Courtney at the beginning. I've learned differently. My sister is lovely inside and out."

An angel descended from Heaven, Adam thought, grappling with all his own doubts.

Curt beat a path through the throng, smiling his incomparable smile. He tapped a firm hand on Adam's shoulder. "I'm back to claim my girl. I can see Courtney standing by herself for a minute, Adam. You'd better not hang around. All the guys think she's terrific."

Curt gathered Darcy in with a sigh of pure joy, bending his head so they were cheek to cheek.

It had been such a marvellous night—Curt was so happy and relaxed—Darcy fretted whether she should tell him what Barbra had said and disturb his mood.

Only Curt knew her so well. He lifted his mahogany head. "Damned if I can't leave you alone for five minutes and you change. What's the matter?"

Darcy explained.

Afterwards Curt gave a mirthless laugh. "What a bitch!" No one but no one was going to spoil this night. He had it all planned. "I think I'll go over and have a few words with her. She's the one with the panda eyes, half in and half out of her dress?"

Darcy backed off. "Please don't start anything, Curt. You're the host. You can't possibly get into an argument. Your mother would be so upset. She's worked so hard."

"Funny, isn't it?" Curt brooded. "I was feeling sublimely happy, as though at long last things were going right, but there's always something. Obviously she wants to hurt you and do Courtney some harm. Nothing out of the ordinary about good old fashioned jealousy."

"That's what Adam said."

"You can't believe it surely?" Curt narrowed his eyes over Darcy's face.

"No but it was a wretched thing to do. I should find Courtney. I can't see her, can you?"

"Find Adam, find Courtney," Curt said, an edge of amusement back in his voice. "You told Adam about this?"

"Yes I did. I trust Adam."

Curt's green eyes sparkled with hard impatience. He could see his dream of an evening slipping away from him. "He's probably gone after Courtney."

"Oh I'm worried," Darcy stopped all pretence of dancing.

"What do you mean?" Curt looked at this woman he loved, sharply.

"There's some odd current there. Something mocking in Adam's eyes when he looks at her. Just let me find Courtney and I'll be back."

"For cryin' out loud!" Curt tried hard to rein his temper in, but he was feeling extreme frustration. He put a steering hand on Darcy's willowy back. "I'll come with you. I'm getting too old for this, girl."

"Tell me that later!" She threw the challenge over her bare shoulder.

It was an answer Curt liked.

Courtney had disappeared.

"She told me she had a headache," Katherine Berenger told them when asked. "I find myself with a tiny one too. Such a lot of *noise* but everyone is enjoying themselves immensely. She's probably popped back to the house for a few minutes."

Half way back to the homestead Curt pulled Darcy off the path and out of view.

"For goodness sake, forget Courtney for a moment, kiss me." He took her face in his hands.

Darcy closed her eyes. For long moments she melted into him and he into her, their bodies galvanised wherever they touched.

"I love you," Darcy breathed on one long voluptuous sigh, arching her throat so he could kiss it. There was no resistance in her only exquisite sensation.

He captured her mouth again, his arms suddenly crushing her.

She didn't complain. She wanted it to last forever. He could devour her if he liked.

Long minutes passed before Darcy stumbled a few steps back.

Curt caught at her arm to steady her. "You want to go after Courtney, right?" He was amazed at his own admirable self-control.

"I think I should."

"One of the things I love about you," he mocked.

They expected to find Courtney in the house. They didn't. She wasn't downstairs and she wasn't in her room.

"No doubt about it, Courtney's an exceptionally tidy girl," Curt remarked, looking with approval around the bedroom where not a thing was out of place.

"Where *is* she?" Darcy, who wasn't the tidiest person in the world, moaned.

"Obviously, my love, she's gone back to dancing," Curt said patiently. "Or Adam wants to make love to her. I could see it in his face. We *all* know I want to make love to you. I'm just comforting myself with the thought there's plenty of time later." He moved in closer and pulled her in to face him. "Courtney's a big girl now."

"Of course she is, but it's not like her to disappear. Maybe she's run off?"

"Don't be ridiculous," Curt groaned and began nuzzling her ear and cheek. "It's our golden opportunity to get away."

She rested against him, thinking the fact he loved her—had loved her for so long—was a miracle.

"I'm absolutely ravenous for you," he said, dropping an exploratory kiss on her mouth.

Perfect! Her lips quivered beneath his. She wanted him to peel her beautiful dress off her. From the fine tremor in his body she knew he could barely stop himself from trying. Desire was starting to consume them. Like fire… They were moving, slowly, sensuously, finding their fit, her breasts to his chest, thighs locked, her long legs parted to accommodate one of his. Oh to be totally alone to make love all night!

Courtney's voice sounded so close it forced its way through their passion. Almost dazedly they broke apart.

"I don't want to discuss it. Why are you acting like this, Adam?"

"Oh hell!" Curt moaned. "I'm going to get the two of us onto an island. This has nothing to do with us."

"Why don't we find out?" Darcy whispered.

Curt squeezed her fingers. "What are you whispering for? It's a lover's tiff surely?"

"They're not lovers," Darcy said. "You've got it all wrong."

Curt's mouth compressed. "Have I? One thing I've learned. Don't argue with you, Darcy."

It was Courtney's clear voice again, raised in temper. "It's *not* true." They could barely hear Adam's reply.

"We'll have to go downstairs," Darcy said, reaching out and banging a cupboard door presumably as a means of alerting them. "This is embarrassing."

"Imagine how *I* feel!" Curt groaned. "An interloper in my own home. Come on, while I'm still able to summon up my last remnant of patience."

Courtney and Adam were standing in the entrance hall. Adam raised a laconic hand as they walked down the grand divided staircase. "Hi!"

Courtney was speechless, her blue eyes like Delft saucers in her young unhappy face.

Darcy hurried down to her. "Kath said you had a headache. We came to find you. Are you okay?" She touched her sister's arm lightly.

"No I'm not." Now that Darcy was there, Courtney relaxed

very slightly. "I never met a worse trouble maker than Barbra Vaughn. She's been having the time of her life bad mouthing me all night. Adam, here—" she swept him with a scalding glance "—couldn't wait to tell me."

"That's not exactly true, Courtney," Adam answered. "Barbra spoke to Darcy. She had quite a bit to say to me too later on. I was actually coming to warn you about her, not to start a fight."

"I'll speak to her," Darcy said, the blood rushing into her cheeks. "I can tell you she won't come off best."

"I'm sure none of us seriously considers she will," Curt laid a calming hand on Darcy's shoulder. "Why don't you let me speak to her. I remind myself I'm the host around here."

"I'm not going to let you go without me," Darcy exclaimed.

"My dearest Darcy, that would be overkill."

Darcy went to answer, but Courtney burst out, "What I want to know is, did anyone *outside* Adam believe her?"

The muscles along Adam's firm jawline tightened. "It's good they don't hang people around here any more," he said, sounding bitterly sarcastic. "You've turned yourself into judge and jury."

Strain showed itself in every line of Courtney's delicate body. "You've been suspicious of me from the first." She turned on him. "You practically accused me of trying to influence my dying father unduly."

"No, no, Courtney," Darcy protested. Not that it hadn't appeared to anyone who didn't know her there might be some grounds for such an accusation.

But Courtney, tormented by Adam's kiss was unstoppable. That kiss had shaken her to the foundations, causing her to indulge in a glass too many of champagne. She shook her head from side to side. "Now Barbra, what a rattlesnake! She's never forgiven me for getting the job. You know the saying. Throw enough dirt and some always sticks."

Darcy surveyed her sister in dismay. Dirt had stuck in the past. She could attest to that.

"Calm down, Courtney," Curt said soothingly. "I promise you I'll deal with this Barbra without making a big thing of it."

"No one has answered me." Courtney looked very near to tears. "Did anything she said get through to you all? I swear I've never discussed my family with anyone. It wasn't a nice story anyway. Cold-blooded abandonment. I certainly didn't entertain my colleagues with how I was going to con my own dying father—" She broke off, deliberately presenting her back to Adam.

A powerful surge of protectiveness swept through Darcy. She went to her very threatened looking sister, wrapping an arm around her. "We didn't believe a word of it! Adam hit it right on the head. It was pure jealousy. Jealousy is one of the deadly sins. I think you owe him an apology."

"No I do *not!*" Courtney was a long way from forgiving Adam. She was, in fact, in a highly emotional state, conflicting feelings boiling through her bloodstream.

"You know where she probably got some of her information from don't you?" Darcy said. "Poor Lara. Another innocent party. She must have schemed to get Lara on side."

"Well you don't need me," Adam started to turn away, his handsome *dark* face hawklike with tension.

"Of course we don't!" Courtney cried. "I think you should look on yourself as being sacked!" Now the tears were starting. "I could see it in your eyes. You believed her. You think I'm a vampire!" she accused him with high drama.

Adam turned back. "Oh cut it out. You don't know what to do, do you, unless you get adoration?" In the very next breath he apologised. "I'm sorry," he said stiffly.

Curt could scarcely credit this was little Courtney. He slung an arm around Adam's shoulders, man to man, it was so much easier—thinking from such splendid beginnings this had turned into a very bumpy night. "Why don't we let Darcy handle this," he suggested. "I could do with a drink."

"Fine in my book," said Adam.

It was a down hill slide after that. A magical evening ended in dashed hopes.

The sisters returned home to Murraree facing certain inescapable facts. It wasn't easy coping with relationships. The traumatic alienation of their childhood and adolescence which they'd thought to be putting behind them had resurfaced in the form of Darcy's niggling doubts. This had the effect of putting Courtney very much on the defensive. She could only think her motivation for returning to Murraree when her father was dying was being silently questioned. In effect, Barbra Vaughn's spiteful lies had put her back on trial. She was not quite the person they believed her to be? Also she'd made a perfect fool of herself—something she tried never to do—and suffered waves of mortification because of it.

Hot tempered Darcy, by the end of that night, a hair's breadth away from explosion, had her own wincing feelings of regret. She had left a frustrated Curt striding away from her as if in the space of twenty four hours he had gone from professing his undying love for her to wanting to strangle her with her own hair.

"First you played hand maiden to your father. Now you're going to hold Courtney's hand," he accused her, storming off. "From where I'm coming from, that's more than enough!"

Equally upset Darcy had hurled after him. "Oh, grow up!" A bizarre thing to say when she had finally made the decision nothing would stand between her and her man.

Even before they'd left Sunset Downs talk had continued to rage about the way Barbra Vaughn had offered unsolicited insights into Courtney's character. Of course Barbra was jealous, they were all in agreement on that. But the degree of influence Courtney had had on the re-making of Jock McIvor's will couldn't be ignored could it? Nor the fact they'd all at some point voiced caution. Few people could achieve what Courtney had achieved in such a short time. She was blessed with exceptional charm. Was she to be blamed for using it for her own advancement?

"Everything Barbra told you was lies!" Courtney protested, believing they were all turning against her. "It was revenge pure and simple."

It wasn't true they were turning against her. All three, Darcy, Curt and Adam were trying to deal with the allegations in their own way. Curt appeared the most convinced, ready to dump the whole issue but Darcy had so many emotions jostling around in her heart it was difficult for her not to go into overdrive. As usual, Curt was the one to bear the brunt of it.

So for the sisters getting back to where they were prior to the polo weekend wasn't all that easy. Neither was as comfortable with the other as they had been. To compound the fraught situation Darcy hadn't heard from Curt for a week, which made her feel utterly wretched. Not only that, anxiety was gnawing away at her regarding her promise to tell him what had caused their dramatic rift.

Back to square one.

Work continued on the restoration. Courtney lost herself in that, hoping and praying things would settle down though she considered she would be on her guard against Adam Maynard always. Darcy went back to her dawn to dusk schedule. For several days now a bull catching team had been operating roughly four miles out. By mid-morning of what turned out to be an eventful day Darcy rode into the second mustering camp where about three hundred cattle, a lot of them cleanskins, were milling about, sending up a pall of red dust. There she caught Sean Davis, the jackeroo, hot-footing it through the rails.

A cheeky grin lit his face when he saw her. "Hi, Boss! Bloody bull nearly got me." He wrested the end of his checked shirt from a piece of barbed wire. "Just made it."

"You've been warned not to do anything foolish, Sean," Darcy settled the mare and walked towards him. "Where's the rest of the team?"

Sean took off his akubra and ran a hand through his tangle of sweat dampened hair. "They'll be back shortly with another mob. Joe and I had been wiring new rails into position, until that mad bull decided I'm outta here."

"You'd better give Joe a hand then," Darcy said, waving at the aboriginal ringer who waved cheerfully back.

"Bloody thing charged a few minutes before you arrived," Sean said as though he was mortally offended by the bull's actions. He swivelled to take another look at the intimidating beast. "Just what I needed after a crook night. He's a real bastard. Doesn't like humans."

"Language, Sean," Darcy said mildly, looking at the "mad bull" in question.

"Sure you weren't antagonising him?"

"Yeah, well..." Sean's tanned cheeks coloured. "I might have yelled olay a couple of times but I wasn't figurin' on that response! How come nothing much seems to happen to the aboriginal guys?"

"For one they don't go around rousing the stock. They exercise caution at all times. Another they're too smart, they're too fast, and they have totems to protect them. Up in the Territory they can swim through crocodile infested waters where you and I would make a lovely meal."

"Maybe it's about time I acquired a totem," Sean said, impressed.

"All you need to do, Sean, is go down a gear."

The large reddish coloured bull was standing its ground in the centre of the holding yard. It still looked furious, snorting violently and pawing the earth. The black tips of its horns carved the air with every movement of its massive head. It bore an uncanny resemblance to the fighting beasts in a bull ring.

Joe, single-mindedly repairing the smashed fence, looked completely unperturbed. Like Darcy he'd been working cattle all his life. A pandemonium of sound in the form of bellows, barking dogs and cracking whips, was coming closer. Darcy turned her head. A distance off through the acacia shrouded timber she could see the other mob spread out. Cleanskins probably. Four riders were behind the cattle, cracking the odd whip, the working cattle dogs, the Blueys, thoroughly enjoying themselves, kept pace beside the mounted stockmen, yapping their heads off, moving the mob along.

"They're back," Darcy said with satisfaction, pointing the jackeroo back to work. "Don't let Tom see you standing around talking, Sean."

"Right, Boss." Sean gave her another one of his cheeky salutes and moved off. It wasn't easy keeping authority over the men. She wasn't surprised after they had worked under her father, but Sean was just a bit of a kid, Darcy thought tolerantly. If he got too cheeky she'd pull him back into line. It was the other new guy, Prentice, who was starting to make her uncomfortable with his looks. She knew her father wouldn't have tolerated those kinds of glances levelled at her. Any man who hadn't shown her the utmost respect was literally out on his ear. She couldn't allow a situation to build up. She couldn't make anything of it either by asking Tom to have a word with him. Prentice might have to go. She should have read the signs at the beginning or had Curt show his presence. Curt was perfect boss material.

The roar of a rapidly approaching vehicle added to the considerable din. A station four-wheel drive with Courtney at the wheel was coming down into the clearing at speed. Darcy was momentarily distracted. What did Courtney want? She didn't often come down to the yards. Next moment she felt her heart miss a beat as Sean yelled loudly: "Darcy, watch out!"

Instinctively Darcy took to her heels, obeying the warning without quite knowing why. She threw a glance back over her shoulder, rocked by what she saw. The monstrous bull, excited by all the noise and confusion, had taken it into its head to mount a second charge It smashed through the standing side fence as though the heavy rails were matchsticks.

There was movement everywhere, a frantic rush to her aid. The stockmen left the mob to surge through the trees. Another stockman on one of the mustering motor bikes burst into the clearing but it was Courtney who in the end valiantly drove the four-wheel drive with its heavy bull bar into the gap between the bull and her running sister.

They all heard the bull's horn rip through metal before it went down.

In the same instant four stockmen converged on the fallen animal its tail flicking back and forth in agitation. Darcy left the men to it. She raced over to the vehicle, her own fright forgotten, only to find Courtney's golden head slumped over the wheel.

CHAPTER ELEVEN

COURTNEY spent almost a week in Koomera Crossing Bush Hospital. She had suffered a concussion that had the hospital chief, Doctor Sarah McQueen worried at the beginning and two cracked ribs. Accidents, even tragedies were a way of life in the bush. Even so Darcy was extremely upset to see her younger sister lying so quietly in a hospital bed. Darcy knew if anything had gone seriously wrong with Courtney she would never have got over it. Courtney's quick action had undoubtedly saved Darcy from injury or worse. That alone overcame all obstacles and drew the sisters close.

At the beginning when Courtney was rambling incoherently it was impossible not to catch the word, *Mum.*

"You know she wants her mother, don't you, Darcy?" Curt had drawn Darcy out into the hospital corridor.

"Yes, yes, I know." She was trembling with reaction.

"So what are you going to do about it?"

"I'm going to get my mother out here. Are you happy?" Darcy had looked up at him with tears in her eyes. "Oh Curt, you just don't know how I feel."

His eyes were compassionate. "I know it'll be hard for you to see your mother after all these years. I also know anything that's good for Courtney you'll allow."

"I haven't begun to thank you," she said. "I'm always amazed the way you turn up when I desperately need you."

Curt shrugged. "I do my best."

The reason Courtney had driven down to the holding yard was because Curt had sent word ahead he would be touching down on Murraree in another thirty minutes. He had a potential buyer lined up for Murraree's Bell helicopter, a pilot and a very skilful mechanic who was prepared to do the work that was needed on the vintage chopper. Courtney knew Darcy would want to be on hand to greet him.

It was Curt who had flown Courtney protected by a neck brace the station's first aid room kept on hand to Koomera Crossing Bush Hospital with the highly anxious Darcy as a passenger. As ever Curt had been a tower of strength. She couldn't imagine life with out him. She also sensed from a certain *stillness* in him she would have to work hard to convince him of that when things settled. Her heart needed him. Her soul needed him. Her body was crying out for him.

The afternoon their mother was to arrive—Curt had made it easy by arranging a charter flight—Darcy made herself scarce. She had promised Courtney a visitor.

"Not Adam?" Courtney, with a livid blue-black-purple bruise on her temple was very still beneath the white coverlet. She gave Darcy a haunting look.

"No, not Adam, though he's rung many times and sent those beautiful flowers." Darcy turned her head to acknowledge the exquisite arrangement.

"Nice of him," Courtney responded, her eyelids lowered. "So who is it?" She couldn't keep what sounded very much like disappointment out of her voice.

"You'll see." Darcy conquered her own feelings to smile. "I promise you're going to feel so much better when your visitor arrives."

* * *

She met Curt later at the pub where she'd been staying during Courtney's time in hospital. It was a miracle he didn't get tired of it all, she thought, but Curt was one of those men destined to help friends and neighbours through all sorts of crises. Courtney was due to be discharged the following morning and Curt was to fly them back home.

"You're going to ask your mother to stay for a few days, aren't you?" he prompted, settling back with an ice cold beer. They were having a late lunch in the very pleasant dining room which served light but surprisingly good meals.

"You should have been a priest," Darcy said, all churned up inside.

"It might have been easier than trying to court you," he retaliated with a crisp edge in his voice. "You can't let her go straight back home. Courtney loves her mother."

"I think it's a bit too much to ask I should love her too," Darcy said and gave a brittle laugh.

"You're suffering either way, Darcy." Curt let his gaze range over her. She had taken to wearing her hair out so it swirled in a dark silken cloud with every movement of her head. She looked tired but impossibly beautiful. Her expression had more than a touch of anguish. He reached across to shake her slender fingers. "Everything will work out, Darcy. It will take a lot from you but it will be worth it in the end. You're being offered a chance at reconciliation. Not just *you.* All of you."

"What if I've got nothing to say?" she whispered, gathering up his strong hand and holding it to her mouth.

"When have you ever had nothing to say?" How her actions confounded him. Time after time.

"This is different. I don't have the heart for it. My mother deserted me."

"Yes she did!" he agreed, "but somehow you've survived."

"I've always had you," she said simply. "I see now I've always drawn strength from *you.* Not Dad."

His smile was faintly twisted. "Who spent his life causing problems and misery. Ah well, he had his time. The future is for us. Eat up, Darcy," he urged briskly. "You're getting way too thin."

"According to the Duchess of Windsor a woman could never be too thin—"

"Or too rich. I know."

Darcy fixed him with her eyes. "Will you come back with me?"

"No." He shook his handsome head. "I'll walk back to the hospital with you and I'll wait in town to say hello to your mother. But you're on your own, my love."

The tender note in his voice after their long week of estrangement made her heart leap in her breast like a fish to the gaff. "Do you know my greatest fear?" she asked, staring deep into his eyes.

"Can I handle it?" Curt's voice was quiet.

"Is that *you* might abandon me," Darcy breathed, from the depths of her being.

For a few moments the small hospital room was locked in silence as though each woman was holding her breath.

"Oh, my God, Darcy!" Tremulously Marian cleared her dry throat. She rose very shakily to her feet, staring intently at her older daughter in a heart broken, loving way. She was desperate to reach out, but Darcy's high mettled expression said very plainly, "Don't crowd me." Marian fought to keep control. It was anguish. Worse that that. She couldn't prevent the emotional tears from pouring down her cheeks. "Darcy!" she whispered, experiencing the deep howling feeling she had lost her daughter forever. This beautiful dark-haired, jewel eyed young woman was a vision. She was tall even with her swan's neck bent, allowing her lustrous hair to act as a protective shield.

"Please sit down again," the vision said, her tone devoid of a daughter's affection, but kind enough. "It must have been a long trip?" Despite the regal demeanour Darcy had inherited from her paternal grandmother, she felt *dazed,* though she would rather have died than admit it. Her mother had scarcely changed for all the years they had been apart. Marian's short blonde hair was beautifully groomed. She had kept her youthful figure. Her delicate features were firm. Her skin was lovely, with scarcely a line. The blue trouser suit she wore with a white tank top was cool and pretty. She had pearls at her ears. A beautiful sapphire and diamond ring threw off light above a white gold wedding band. The diamond solitaire Jock McIvor had given Marian, as big as a man's thumbnail was still in its box in the homestead safe.

Courtney would look like this at the same age, Darcy thought. But Darcy knew in her heart Courtney was stronger. Courtney wouldn't allow a man to rule her life. Courtney wouldn't forsake her child. Darcy was more than willing to take a huge bet on that.

"I want to thank you for letting me come," Marian was saying in her gentle voice that was so much like Courtney's. She resumed her bedside seat, grasping her younger daughter's hand for moral support.

"Courtney wanted you," Darcy said as though that explained it. "Even when she was badly concussed she was murmuring your name."

"I can't tell you how glad I am to be here," Marian turned back to Darcy. "It was so good of you. I know what my being here involves for you, Darcy."

"I doubt that you do," Darcy shook her head. "But welcome anyway. We're expecting Courtney to be discharged tomorrow morning. I'm sure you'd like to stay on at the homestead for a while to be with her. Courtney would like you to see all the work that's been done. She's played quite a hand in that."

Courtney's reaction was almost pitiful in its joy. "You mean Mum can come back home?" she asked as though that was all she had ever wanted.

"That's what I said." Darcy smiled down at her sister. "How are the ribs?"

"Okay so long as no one tries to hug me," Courtney lay very quietly, but her eyes were blazing. "I don't want to get too carried away, but I've dreamed of this day even if I had to get knocked unconscious for it to happen. The three of us together." Her small face looked so indescribably tender and sweet Darcy bent to kiss her.

"You're a heroine!"

Courtney swallowed back tears of joy. "You'd do the same for me."

"You bet I would!" Darcy said. "I know it's cured Sean of play-acting at being a bull fighter. Getting and holding onto good men is difficult and Sean needs a lot of training. He doesn't yet know how to read the country or handle cattle. The love of adventure doesn't make one a bushman. But we agree on one thing. Neither of us wants to see that particular bull ever again."

The meeting lasted almost an hour. It couldn't have been called a great success. It wasn't bathed in the radiance of reconciliation. Darcy chose not to respond beyond politeness to her mother's overtures. She allowed Courtney to do the talking. But the meeting couldn't be judged a failure either. Darcy had in her fashion acknowledged her mother. Marian's defection had in so many ways stolen Darcy's childhood. She had been left with deep emotional wounds in exchange. Deep wounds needed time to heal. Yet Courtney's chance accident as upsetting as it was had played an important part in changing their lives. It had opened the door on a better future.

Life continued. It was time for the big muster.

The wilder cattle, the rogues, liked to hide out in the curving, twisting maze of lignum swamps running across the station. There they could ignore the noisy helicopters that hovered in the royal-blue sky above them. Cattle weren't stupid. The older ones had learned choppers might make a frightening din but they couldn't actually *touch* them. Consequently driving the bullocks out of the swamps and getting them to the yards, ultimately to the market place was a never ending problem.

The previous couple of days Darcy had been using a chartered helicopter along with its pilot. The station helicopter had been sold thanks to Curt and his wide circle of contacts, but as yet time was limited for Darcy and Curt as trustee and experienced adviser to take a trip to the city to buy a replacement. The charter pilot had worked in the vast riverine desert called the Channel Country many times before, but he had never worked on Murraree. As a result there were lots of difficulties with air to ground communications. Often Tom and the men were left guessing what the pilot intended to do. On two occasions, valuable time had been lost when the pilot started pushing the cattle in the wrong direction. It was a very expensive operation and not proving all that successful.

This put Darcy in the position of asking Curt for yet another favour. Sunset Downs had two helicopters. Could she borrow one just for the day?

"I hope you're not thinking of going up yourself?" he'd asked, just as she knew he would. "It's dangerous work."

"And I can do it."

"Noted, but I prefer you didn't. I'll arrange something. If necessary I'll come myself."

Darcy couldn't hide her relief. In the long months McIvor had been ill rogue cattle had become something of a problem. These weren't docile beasts that could be driven back to the yards without much trouble. These were wild animals so desperate to get away and so fast in full flight, it was easier to let some go rather than exhaust stockmen and horses in giving chase. It was endless back breaking work in sizzling heat. The Northern wet season was coming up. It was quite possible the station would swap near drought conditions for floods. The pioneering era in the great Outback was by no means over, Darcy thought hanging on herself by sheer grit and determination.

She was making her way back to the homestead, bone weary but so glad Curt himself was bringing in the chopper that morning. Although Curt's much loved father had lost his life in a helicopter crash there was no option but for all station owners to continue to use the "humming birds" for easy transport and cattle mustering. Darcy had mustered with the men for years, camped out with them, but always with her father present. In that respect McIvor had always acted as her supreme protector. Surprisingly McIvor hadn't handled the chopper as well as she did when she'd hit her stride but she'd watched Curt working cattle many times and had to concede he was the master.

Across her path a party of emus, maybe twenty, Australia's great flightless birds, trod their way majestically through the silver sea of mirage, dipping their long necks and their tail plumes at the noise of the approaching jeep. As she drove nearer they took off on their long sturdy legs doing she judged around fifty klms an hour. She had clocked them at speed doing sixty and keeping pace with the jeep but they quickly tired

She was entering the main compound when she recognised the new stockman, Prentice, coming out of the men's quarters. She couldn't understand that at all. He should have been out with the others. She brought the jeep to a halt calling out to him: "Hey, Prentice! Shouldn't you be out with the others?"

He turned very slowly, eyeing her in his unsettling manner. "Well if it isn't Lady Boss."

"Ms. McIvor to you," Darcy said briskly. "You haven't answered my question."

"And what *was* that again?" He walked towards her, holding onto her with his unshifting gaze.

"Well you've got about a minute to answer," Darcy clipped off.

"I'll say this for yah," he laughed, coming right up to the open jeep and resting his calloused hand on the door. "You're cool, real cool. That's what attracted me to you in the first place. 'Course you're beautiful too."

"I think you'd better stop right there." Darcy stared back at him not making the mistake of showing the faintest sign of weakness, let alone encouragement. "Go on your way. And go *now!*"

"So Ms. McIvor expects to be obeyed without argument or question?"

His tone was so aggressive, Darcy bridled. "Indeed I do. That's if you want to hold onto your job." She forced herself to look back into his deep set dark eyes. He was tall, broad shouldered, his body formidably fit. In other words, he was potentially dangerous.

"It looks like I've used up my time here already," he confessed. "McLaren doesn't want me around."

"Tom told you to come back?"

He nodded. "Bloody old fool! All because I chose to kick a horse."

"I'm sure you've forgotten to mention the ferocity of the kick," Darcy accused coldly. "Tom wouldn't sack you for nothing."

"*You* could overturn his decision," he suggested, a strange look of excitement in his eyes.

"You're joking," Darcy told him brusquely. "If Tom McLaren saw fit to dismiss you his decision stands. Pack your things. I want you off my property."

"And how am I going to get off, Lady?" he drawled.

"You rode in. Ride out," she said, her voice sharp and authoritative.

"It's a helluva long thirsty trip to any kind of civilisation," he broke in.

"There's permanent water. There's bush tucker. You had a job but you've been pushing it since the day you arrived." With considerable relief Darcy was aware a chopper had landed somewhere in the vicinity but Prentice appeared so focused on her he hadn't even blinked much less looked around.

"Lookin' at you, you mean?" His breathing was audible. Now he lifted a hand and deliberately stroked her cheek. "It's glossy like warm satin. I didn't realize how starved for a woman I was until I saw you." His eyes moved to her breasts.

"Don't force me to call for help," Darcy warned, her eyes flaring.

"What your little sister?" He gave a laughing grunt. "Pretty little thing but if I had to choose it'd be *you!* You're definitely a fighter. I like fight in a woman."

Darcy felt the anger rise in her chest. "Get the hell out of here," she gritted, her voice deadly serious.

"When I'm thinkin' of pluckin' up the courage to kiss you?" He leaned in towards her, his expression so *awful,* so lustful Darcy knew straightaway she had trouble. "No matter what happens I'll be able to say I kissed Ms. Darcy McIvor of Murraree Station. That's my girl. Turn up those lovely lips of yours," he urged. "Anyone ever tell yah they're luscious!"

Darcy's hand shot out like a jack knife, cracking across his jaw. "You want to get off Murraree alive?" she threatened, adrenalin firing her blood.

He stared at her unperturbed. In fact as she could see, turned on. "Lady, you can't bullshit me. I'm just living for the moment." Painfully he grasped her chin turning up her face to him.

Darcy threw her head back, realizing with utter fury how physically vulnerable a woman was in a man's hands. She was all set to rasp her nails across his face. If she could get on her feet she could use some of the defensive moves she had mastered. Even then she didn't expect to hold off a strong man like Prentice for long.

Up close, he reeked of cigarettes and dry sweat. "This is your last chance, Prentice. Let me go!" she ordered grimly.

"You're wastin' your time, sweetheart," he jeered, savouring the fire in her. "There's no one around to protect yah!"

"Isn't there?" From behind them a man's voice lashed out like a whip. "Move away from the jeep."

Prentice backed off immediately, giving Darcy the opportunity to scramble out of the vehicle. She ran to Curt, laying her hand on his arm. He didn't appear to notice. "It's Prentice, the new man."

"The guy you hired?" He didn't look at her. He kept his eyes on the other man.

Did he have to make it sound like she had exercised terrible judgment? Which as it turned out she had.

"Seriously, there's nuthin' much wrong here, Mr. Berenger." Prentice tried to hide his dismay behind a swaggering bravado. The last thing he wanted was to take a crack at Berenger whose position and exploits were well known to him. For one thing he'd get the life pounded out of him. For another, he'd never find work again. "I was just tellin' Ms McIvor how beautiful she is."

"What an extremely foolhardy thing to do," Curt rasped, his face set and dark. "Go up to the homestead, Darcy." His brilliant gaze raked her briefly. "There's a little situation here that needs to be addressed. I'll join you shortly."

He looked so menacing, so much like a tiger ready to spring, Darcy was afraid he might inflict injury on the stockman. "Don't waste time on him, Curt," she begged.

He continued to ignore her. "Stay exactly where you are,

Prentice," he ordered, as the other man started to back away. "Get back in the jeep, Darcy and drive away. Do it *now!*"

His tone gave her no other option but to obey. "Tom sacked him," she called, getting behind the wheel.

"Top marks for Tom!" Curt responded very tightly. "Before you go, I'm sure Prentice here wants to apologise to you."

"Sure do," Prentice responded in a contrite, strangled voice. "Just a bit of fun. If I've offended you, Ms. McIvor, I'm sorry."

"Just a little bit louder," Curt ordered.

"I'm sorry, ma'am." Prentice put lung power into it.

Darcy didn't answer. If Curt hadn't turned up who knows what Prentice might have tried. He'd been brimming with intention. Ready to force her. The men might have gone after him afterwards, but it was easy to hide away in the bush.

"You should never, *ever,* have chosen Ms. McIvor as a victim," Curt said.

Darcy couldn't bear to stay. She switched on the ignition, pulling away in a cloud of dust.

She found Courtney and their mother sitting comfortably together in the old conservatory which had been turned into a marvellous Garden Room during the restoration. There were new furnishings and fabrics she and Courtney had helped choose, ceramic sculptures, striking animal figurines, and desert palms in huge pots. There was even a fountain quietly playing.

Courtney and their mother were extremely close Darcy had come to see, thinking she and Marian had gone way beyond the time when even a fraction of that closeness could be reestablished.

As she entered the room they both looked up with smiles that quickly faded after one glance at her face. "Everything okay?" Courtney asked anxiously. "You look upset."

"Nothing much." Darcy shrugged, ashamed of herself for wanting comfort. "One of the stockmen forgot his place."

"My dear!" Marian looked perturbed.

"Not that Prentice?" Courtney asked perceptively, with a shudder. "He gives me the creeps. I think you should sack him."

Darcy paced about, pale beneath her golden tan. "Tom has already done that. Seems he mistreated one of the horses."

"I can see him doing that," Courtney said. "What did he try on you, the scumbag?"

"Nothing. I told you." Darcy shook her head.

"He obviously upset you," Marian ventured, thinking Darcy wouldn't bow like she had to any man's will.

"Well he's about to get more than he bargained for." Darcy gave a brittle laugh. "Curt arrived at precisely the right moment for me, the wrong one for Prentice. I left them to it."

"Oh goodness!" There was half triumph, half dismay in Courtney's eyes. "I wouldn't like to be in Prentice's shoes."

"I just hope Curt knows when to stop," Darcy agonized. "I don't think I've ever seen him so furious."

"Surely you're not concerned for that man's safety?" Marian asked. "He was begging for trouble."

"I'm concerned for Curt," Darcy said. "He's coming up to the house then we're going back to the muster. He brought the chopper."

"We heard it land," Courtney said. "There's nothing he wouldn't do for you."

"Sometimes I think I'm pushing him too far," Darcy murmured, checking her graceful stride to stare at her mother and sister.

"Here, sit down, Darcy," Marian said, in a voice full of motherly concern. She rose to her feet and pointed to a chair. "I'll go make coffee. You look like you could do with a cup. I'm sure Curt will like one too. Then you can be on your way."

The men hadn't a moment's difficulty following Curt's orders on the ground or his manoeuvres in the air. How strong was a man's authority, Darcy thought, revelling in it in one way and vaguely galled by it in another. As a woman she had to fight hard for authority. She'd been certain she could deal with most things and she could, but just being a woman posed safety problems with fools like Prentice around.

"What did you do to him?" She had asked a stern faced Curt later.

"You mean before I kicked his butt? Don't worry, Darcy. You won't see him again."

They kept going right through the day, until suddenly they were all exhausted.

"Boy am I gunna sleep tonight!" Sean, the jackeroo, stretched his long lanky frame. "Mr. Berenger is *awesome.* He got them out of every last hidey hole."

"What's left we don't want," Tom McLaren confirmed, happily. "You want to rest, Darcy," he said, looking over at her as she lounged against a tree trunk. "You look near exhausted, but there's no point in arguing with you. We could never have accomplished all we've done, without Curt."

"Don't I know it," she sighed.

"This work is too tough, too physically draining for you," Tom said, worried. "With your mother here I thought you'd have a chance to rest."

"Don't want to rest, Tom."

"I worry about you, that's all," Tom mumbled. He looked up, his expression lightening as he glanced past Darcy. "There you are, Curt. We've got billy tea."

"Don't ask me to get it," Darcy said, trembling with fatigue.

"You push yourself too hard," Curt commented, accepting a steaming mug of tea from Tom.

"That's what I've been tellin' her," Tom said. "She's tryin' to tread in her dad's footsteps."

"I feel fine," Darcy muttered, crossly.

"Stand up," Curt dared her.

"I will in a few minutes."

He slumped down beside her, crossing his long legs in front of him. "Don't ask me how *I* feel," he complained.

"You're Superman," she said, not fighting the urge to lay her head on his shoulder.

"Even Superman needs a rest," Curt offered, dryly. "Let me know when you're ready to get to your feet."

Afterwards Darcy never quite knew how it happened but she found herself walking out the door with Curt, an overnight bag in tow. Marian and Courtney stood on the verandah waving them off. Mother and daughter had had long serious talks during Marian's stay. Both were perfectly well aware of the powerful bond between Darcy and Curt. It went far beyond the sexual attraction it was obvious each had for the other. It was only natural they needed time together. Kath Berenger could be depended upon to make herself scarce Marian thought. Darcy had had so much unhappiness forced on her she deserved all the love and comfort in the world.

When they arrived on Sunset Darcy walked into the grand entrance hall calling, "Kath, are you there?" It suddenly occurred to her Curt hadn't contacted his mother to say he was bringing her back. Not that Kath didn't always make her very welcome. She and Curt's mother had always been in tune. Darcy started towards the grand staircase that wound into the upper gallery: "Kath, hello?"

Darcy strained hard to hear an answer.

Curt a few moments behind her, came through the door. "Where's your mother?" she asked, throwing him a glance.

His green eyes provided the answer she needed. "In Sydney." He kept his voice, matter-of-fact, even businesslike.

"You were a long time telling me," she protested, turning full on to face him. "Where's Stacey then?" Stacey was

Sunset's long time housekeeper, cum companion, cum family friend. Stacey usually came out to meet her.

"Stacey went with Mum." Curt's handsome head was tilted slightly. "You know how she fancies herself as Mum's lady-in-waiting. They're having a few days on the town. They'll be meeting up with Aunty Pat."

"So you got me over here under false pretences?"

"Just the two of us," he said.

She stared at him. "You sound very serious."

He closed the double front doors with their beautiful fanlights and sidelights and locked them. "If you don't want to stay with me, you'd better start hollering now."

"It all depends what you intend?" She had an overwhelming desire to tease him.

His eyes glinted. "Right at this moment I need to soak in a hot tub. My muscles ache. Then I intend to feed you. After that, who knows?"

Curt was luxuriating in his deep man-size bath when he became aware Darcy was standing in the doorway. She was wearing a silky robe, white as shimmering snow. The outline of her body showed through. As a startling contrast her magnificent sable mane fanned out around her face, over her shoulders and onto the silk. She carried a small cut glass bottle of bath salts in her hands for all the world like a geisha making an offering.

"May I join you?" she whispered. Her beautiful eyes were enormous, the black pupils dilated.

Sexual excitement poured through Curt's hard muscled body like a torrent. He was astounded she had come to him. Her being there so obviously naked beneath her robe filled him with an emotion he identified as exultation.

"Please." He held out his hand, sucking his breath in as she let the robe fall to her feet.

Her body was beautiful. Perfect. Only he could see it. He

ached for it. She was giving him a gift more precious than diamonds, rubies and emeralds piled as high as a mountain. She was giving him herself. Winning Darcy McIvor was the one thing in his life he had almost despaired of. Now he saw very clearly she needed him as much as he needed her.

"I love your being here," he said, conscious there was a faint tremor in his voice.

"I love being here."

He moved blindly raising his splendid body out of the water. "Come here to me."

She gave him a smile so sweet it was ravishing. "I want to perfume the water. Do you mind?"

"It's the one thing we need." He took the cut glass container from her scattering the pink bath salts into the tub.

Immediately the perfume rose like an overflow of wildflowers. He lent her a supporting hand while Darcy put one long slender leg then the other into the scented water. They sank deep together at the same end, the fragrant, pink tinged water lapping around them.

Darcy lay back sighing deeply. Curt's strong arms encompassed her. Her head rested back against his shoulder, her eyelids fluttering. Her long hair when wet, was like glistening ebony. Locks trailed over her breasts. His mouth moving over hers infused her with desire. She felt his warm lips slide down the long sweep of her neck, over the slope of her shoulder, his tongue gathering up the beads of water that lay along her skin.

Now his strong brown hands caressed her breasts, sleek from the water, the nipples clustered, a deep pink colour. He moved lingeringly over her wet flesh, his fingertips stroking the curves, the planes and secret dells of her body. The most tender spots. It raised a storm of emotion in her.

Curt felt her involuntary shivers. Her head was pressed back hard into his chest. Her lovely taut buttocks circled his groin, his sex rock hard and heavy with arousal. He wanted her so badly a deep groan was wrenched from him. He rotated her body so she was lying on top of him, thrusting into her because he couldn't take any more sensation. He was frantic for release.

Darcy's nails were scrapping along his back. She didn't mean to hurt him. She couldn't help it. She manoeuvred herself into the best possible position, settling on his lap, her agonized little cries urging him on. "Yes, yes, I love it!" She directed her trembling hands to his body, wanting to give him double the pleasure he was giving her, if that were possible. She let her mouth descend on his, as passionate as any kiss could be. Surely the water in the tub should be *boiling?*

Curt could feel her inner muscles begin to spasm. She was gasping, throwing back her head muttering something beyond his hearing, but the message was clear. Engulfed by sensation he gripped her beautiful body pulling her deeper and deeper into him.

Sublime.

He heard her cry his name, as high and tremulous as a bird.

Now!

In the predawn they quit the house exiting by the kitchen door and making their way to the stables where they saddled up and rode out into their brave new world. They had made love in a scented tub; by starlight entwined in Curt's bed, hearts beating as one, then finally after hours of refreshing sleep when they awoke to dawn's misty light and the great orchestra of birds that was starting to tune up.

At their favourite haunt buried deep in the virgin bush, Curt wrapped her in his arms. "I've got something for you," he said, his vibrant voice husky with emotion.

She looked into his beloved face, thinking she was to be freed of the bonds of loneliness forever. "What is it?" she asked softly.

He leaned forward to kiss her soft, warm lips. "I want

to announce our love to the world. I can't wait for Christmas." He dipped into his breast pocket, pulling out a dark blue velvet box. His eyes glittered with resolution. "This is your engagement ring, Darcy McIvor who's led me a merry dance in more ways than one. The engagement ring I bought you too long ago. I want you to wear it. I want everyone to know I love you and you love me. You do love me, don't you?"

Her eyes pooled with tears. This was the moment to risk everything. Tell him. Be completely honest. "I've loved you since I was a little girl," she said. "But I've been hiding things from you, Curt."

"I know," he answered gravely, his arm encircling her to lend her strength. "But you're going to tell me now?"

She nodded, hoping with all her heart the truth would set her free. "I must. The fact I haven't told you has tormented me every day of the years since it happened." She gave him an uncertain look. "I had a miscarriage, Curt. I lost our baby."

Right in front of her he visibly paled. "Good God!" His voice was very quiet but it commanded all her attention. It sounded like she had shot him with a gun and he was in terrible pain.

They'd been half lying back on the sand, now he sat ramrod straight. "And you didn't tell me?" He looked back at her incredulously, his shock apparent. "Do you realise how very far from normal that is? I had the right to be told." He sounded implacable.

"I know. I know!" She reached out to grasp his arm. Found it unyielding."But I had reason to believe you'd been unfaithful."

"Unfaithful?" He pulled away from her sharply, his eyes flashing with anger.

"Dad had you followed." Her face twisted with shame. "It was that last trip you took to Sydney. He hired a private investigator to follow you around."

"So?" Curt queried bitterly, his green eyes glittering like glass. "There couldn't have been a bloody thing the man had to report."

"He took several photographs of you with a beautiful girl." Darcy continued doggedly. "You were obviously involved. I'm not a complete fool. The camera didn't lie."

Curt looked like he had no idea what she was talking about. "Where are these photographs?" he demanded, his finely cut nostrils flaring. "What have you done with them?"

"I have them," she said, quivering in reaction. "Many times I've tried to throw them away but I couldn't. There's not a shadow of doubt you had strong feelings for her."

"Really?" His voice cracked with sarcasm. "It's a pity someone didn't tell me. But forget the bloody photographs," he gritted. "They're not important. Why didn't you tell me you were pregnant? That was momentous news. I had every right to know."

"I didn't know myself, Curt," she said in a careful voice. "It was early days. There were no obvious signs. The photographs upset me terribly. I don't have to tell you of all people how damaged I already was. I'd been in the saddle all day. I barely made it home. That's when it happened."

He continued to stare at her as if he had never seen her before in his life. "Did your father know?"

"Never!" She shook her head vehemently. "I got myself over to Koomera Crossing. Doctor McQueen looked after me."

Curt let out a strangled breath. "I can't take this in. You've lived with this for four years. I bet Sarah McQueen urged counselling?"

"No, Curt. She understood. There was nothing wrong with me other than a deep sense of betrayal and the grief at the loss of our child."

"Darcy!" he moaned hopelessly, holding his head with his hands. "You've known me all your life. You knew how much

I loved you yet you couldn't turn to me at such a time. I don't know if I can forgive you."

"You *have to!*" she cried, feeling great tremors of fear. "I'd lost the baby by the time you got home." She gave a harsh painful sob.

"You gave me no chance to comfort you." Muscles worked along his jaw. "You didn't tell me. It was my baby too."

She was afraid to touch him in case he flinched away. "I couldn't cope with your wanting another woman," she admitted with much sorrow. "I would never have cheated on you."

"Oh, Darcy!" His voice was a deep groan. "You're talking so wildly. How could I be meeting up with some other girl when I'd just bought this ring? Look at it, damn it. It's a jewel just like your eyes." He opened the discarded velvet box and withdrew a ring. A glorious aquamarine of many carats, flanked on either side by shoulders of diamonds.

"Don't Curt, please." From flamelike happiness to sadness.

"You're going to wear it," he said fiercely, suddenly grabbing her hand and pushing the ring down over her finger. "What a little fool you are. I never betrayed you. I loved you. I still love you, God help me."

"So who was the beautiful girl in the photographs?" she cried hoarsely, dashing her hand across her eyes. "You've no idea how Dad tormented me. Day in and day out. He said if I married you I'd have a lifetime of knowing you had other women on the side."

"Stop now, Darcy," Curt bid her very quietly. "What a devil Jock McIvor really was. I don't know who this girl was. There was no girl." His strongly marked eyebrows swooped together in a frown. "There was never anyone but you." He stared at the glittering pool, the skin over his sculpted cheekbones taut. "Wait a minute." Abruptly he leapt to his feet, towering over her as she languished on the sand. "There was only one girl it could possibly be. Tell me about her?" he said urgently. "Did she have long dark hair and a lovely smile. Very slender. Rather like you in build only several inches shorter?"

"Coltish," Darcy said. "She had a look of springtime and joy. Such joy!"

"Good grief!" Curt's vibrant voice suddenly lacked strength. "It had to be Genny. Genevieve Taylor. She's Aunty Pat's granddaughter. You never did get to meet her but surely you've heard about her? I remember now. Genny had just won a big scholarship to the Juilliard in New York. She was thrilled out of her mind. Genny's a very gifted young violinist. New York is her home now. She's already launched on a career. Genny, my God!" He stared down at Darcy as though he couldn't endure a bigger mistake. "But Genny was just a kid then. Surely you saw that? All of sixteen. The only schoolgirl I ever went around with was you."

Darcy brought herself upright. "All I saw was she was young and beautiful and that you loved her." Her voice was strangled by tears.

"I think very fond of her will do. Darcy, she's *family.* If only you'd shown me or my mother the photographs. The whole sorry mess could have been cleared up."

"So my instincts were all wrong!" She was crying now but wiping away the tears with fierce determination. "I was so much in love I couldn't think straight. All those hormones raging around in my system. Then the miscarriage. It was hard not to believe it was something I did wrong. But I swear I didn't know, Curt. I didn't."

"Ah, Darcy!" He made no effort to hide his distress.

"Afterwards when you came back it was unspeakable. I know I said over and over again I didn't want to see you any more but I was devastated beyond all healing. There seemed no future for us. I thought you were in another relationship you weren't going to tell me about. I'd lost the baby. Dad didn't know about that. He was cruel. Gloating. He was so jealous of you. What you stood for in my life. You were going to take me away and then he would have been truly on his own. His women meant nothing."

The pain in her voice resounded in Curt's heart. "That sonofabitch," he said, his expression hard and condemning. "It all comes back to him."

"I thought he was trying to protect me even if I hated the way he went about it."

"He tried to ruin your life."

"I see that, Curt. "What do you want me to say? I'm sorry, so sorry. But I've suffered." Her voice was stripped of all hope.

"That's what *I* hate. *You* suffering." With purposeful urgency he lifted her to him. Pulled her close. Held her fiercely. "I love you, Darcy," he said. "You're all I want on this earth. I won't ever leave you again." He bent and kissed her wet cheeks. "I always knew you had some unassailable secret. I knew your father played a part in it. I'd even considered the unimaginable but I knew it wasn't so. Jock McIvor had crossed many boundaries but never that."

"Oh no, no!" Darcy exclaimed in horror. "How could you think anything so monstrous?"

"I didn't. But it was something powerful. You wouldn't confide in me."

"I've paid dearly for it," she said, burrowing her head against him. "Forgive me, Curt, for ever doubting you."

"I guess I will in time." He pulled back her hair and stared into her beautiful drowned eyes. "And to think Jock called for me in his hour of need. Isn't life just too strange? I had to see him in his grave before he'd let you go. All I've ever wanted Darcy is to love and protect you. Take care of you. But you had to suffer the loss of our child by yourself."

"I see I deserved it now." Her voice was full of sadness.

"No! Hush!" He hugged her tighter, emphatically shaking

his head. "Never say that. These things happen. Your secret is out now. It had to come out some time."

"I'd just as soon die than have Kath know the whole pitiful story," she murmured.

"Mum doesn't have to know," he reassured her. "It's *our* business. Mum can't wait for us to be married. She can't wait for grandchildren."

Darcy met his eyes directly, thanking God it was so. "Doctor Sarah assured me I could have other children."

"Of course you can. Of course you will." He kissed her passionately. "But I need you to myself for a while. We've got an awful lot of loving to get in."

"Then let's go home," she said.

The light caught the dazzle of her beautiful ring. She could have worn it years ago. But at that moment it seemed doubly precious.

The sun rose higher in a deepening blue sky, a great golden ball that flooded the bush with light. Flocks of birds having given their concert rose screeching and chattering above the trees in multicoloured waves. A dazzling sight in flight. The surface of the dark green lagoon crowded with the sacred blue lotus, was touched with sparkling points of light.

The beauty of it! A pair of mating blue brolgas seized that precise moment to make their appearance, touching down in the shallows with a series of quick running steps After a few moments like a wonderful omen they broke into their enchanting ballet.

Curt turned up her face to him, his green eyes lit by little flames. "We're one, you and I, Darcy. Like the brolgas we mate for life."

"My cup of joy is overflowing," she said.

EPILOGUE

THAT Christmas proved to be the happiest period of the McIvor women's lives. Darcy made no objection when Courtney asked if their mother and her husband Peter could join them on Murraree for the festive season.

Why not? There was no place in Darcy's life now for insoluble problems. What she had learned from Curt was, problems had to be worked through to find a solution. From now on she had to go about reestablishing a new, loving relationship with her mother. In her utterly blissful state Darcy didn't find it at all difficult to move on. Both Marian and Courtney had received the news of her engagement to Curt with unfeigned delight. On all the evidence both women's view was this was a partnership that would *last*.

"I believe it with all my heart," Marian told her elder daughter, compulsively hugging her.

The weekend before Christmas had been set aside for the engagement festivities which took place on Murraree. The festivities lasted right through the weekend, starting with a picnic race meeting, followed by a banquet in Murraree's newly refurbished formal dining room, with a magnificent barbecue the following day to which everyone on both stations, Murraree and Sunset was invited.

Hundreds and hundreds of photographs were taken.

Everyone wanted a record of that marvellous weekend. The wedding was planned for June when the weather would be crisp and beautiful. It also allowed time to decide on Murraree's future. Courtney had made it known she was well content to stay. But everyone was in agreement she couldn't stay on her own.

"I don't believe she'll be on her own for long," was another one of Curt's cryptic comments which he made smiling knowingly to himself.

Darcy knew he meant Adam but she couldn't for the life of her see how that was going to happen. Courtney's and Adam's relationship was really complicated. Both drew a strong response from the other. Anyone could see that, but it appeared beneath the perverse attraction and the good manners, lay an inherent sensitivity that Darcy thought could pretty well be described as *antagonism.* Nevertheless Adam who had a powerful position in their lives was invited to everything as a matter of course. Shaky as the relationship was between Courtney and Adam, Adam got on famously with Marian who took to him on sight.

"So charming. So clever. Such a gentleman!" she purred.

Courtney took care to make her barbed retorts to Darcy when their mother was safely out of earshot.

No, thought Darcy, somewhat regretfully, for she really liked Adam, Courtney and Adam were *not* a perfect match. Her beloved was dreaming.

As Destiny would have it they were all assembled on the verandah enjoying a cold drink when more unresolved business literally landed on their doorstep. Marian and Peter were staying on for a few more days, but Adam was due back at work the following Monday. He was scheduled to leave in the morning with Curt and Darcy who were taking a trip to Brisbane to buy Murraree's new helicopter.

It was getting on to late afternoon and they were idly discussing recent events when a dust covered, badly battered four-wheel drive swept into view. Puzzled Darcy stood up. "Who's that? We're not expecting anyone, are we?" Between Christmas and New Year Murraree had enjoyed a stream of visitors and well wishers. Nothing was ever said, but Murraree was judged to be a good place to visit now that Big Jock McIvor had gone to his reward.

"Whoever it is, they're in one hell of a hurry." Curt joined Darcy at the balustrade, putting his arm around her shoulder. "You'd swear there was a posse in pursuit."

"Could be he wants to arrive before his vehicle falls apart," Adam commented. "It looks like it belongs on the scrapheap."

"Well we're going to find out soon enough." Courtney, too stood up. For some reason her nerves were twitching and it wasn't just Adam's half thrilling, half satirical presence.

The driver of the four-wheel drive not content to park off the circular drive brought the noisy vehicle to a shuddering halt a few feet from the base of the front steps.

"It's not a *man,*" Courtney said, clutching her throat.

Adam shot her a quick glance. "What's wrong?" He rose to standing, frowning at her vaguely fatalistic expression.

"I have a feeling this is *serious,*" Courtney said.

It was Curt who called: "Hello there! Who are you? What do you want?" He didn't demand it. He spoke in a completely nonthreatening voice.

The driver stepped out of the vehicle and slammed the door so hard they all expected it to fall off. She—for it was a *she*—scanned these rich, handsome people, ranged together on the verandah of the heritage listed homestead.

"Which one of you is Darcy?" she responded, in a bone dry, sarcastic voice. She didn't back off but moved further towards them, pausing only to sweep off her wide brimmed hat. The movement released a long silken bolt of glorious copper hair.

"My God!" Recognition came from a deep place inside Darcy. It flowed over her like hot oil. The resemblance was so stunning it left little room for doubt. There was the height. She was taller than Darcy—maybe 5-11—and had whipcord grace. She wore a khaki bush shirt and skin tight jeans. High boots. Her legs went on forever. The leonine mane was a dazzling red-gold. Sapphire eyes blazed up at them with familiar aggression. She even had a dimple in her chin. Her appearance couldn't have been more unnerving.

Darcy didn't have the slightest doubt this was one of McIvor's chickens come home to roost. Hadn't she always known it in her bones? This was Jock's daughter. A McIvor. A knot formed itself in her stomach. Worked up to her throat.

A few feet from Darcy, Courtney stood like a marble figurine, remembering how her father had looked when she was a child. Marian's eyes too had widened in disbelief.

"Cat caught your tongue?" The sapphire gaze honed in on Darcy like her antennae had made the choice. She gave Darcy a bright challenging smile. "Hi, I'm Casey. Jock McIvor was my dad. Now are you going to let me up?"

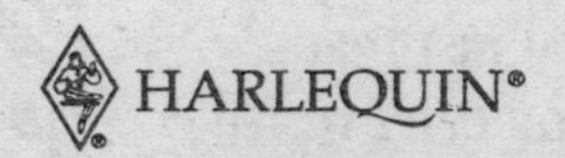

HARLEQUIN ROMANCE®

Coming Next Month

#3863 MARRIAGE AT MURRAREE Margaret Way

Discovering her father was a billionaire cattle king makes Casey McGuire one of the famous "McIvor heiresses." She's worked hard all her life, but she's never had the prospect of money—until now. Nor has she ever truly known love, but irresistible Troy Connellan is ready to change all that. Can wary Casey let go of her past for a future with a rich, powerful—gorgeous—man?

The McIvor Sisters

#3864 WINNING BACK HIS WIFE Barbara McMahon

Heather's ex-husband is back! Hunter never understood why Heather walked out. Even when she confesses the truth, it seems too much has happened for a reconciliation. But Heather can see the attraction is still there—and, deep down, so is the love....

#3865 JUST FRIENDS TO...JUST MARRIED Renee Roszel

Kimberly Albert's boyfriend has just walked out and she needs the one man who's always been there for her: her best friend, Jaxon Gideon. But Jax can't be Kim's shoulder to cry on—he's in love with her. So he decides that if he can't have Kim in his life, he wants her out of it! But Kim's starting to see a new side to Jax—an irresistible, sexy side—and she likes what she sees!

#3866 IMPOSSIBLY PREGNANT Nicola Marsh

Keely Rhodes can't believe her luck when gorgeous Lachlan Brant hires her to design a new Web site for his radio show. The girls at the office think Lachlan is Keely's perfect man, and they tell her to go for it! But after Keely's business/pleasure trip away, she's got more gossip—what she'd thought impossible has happened: she's pregnant with Lachlan's baby!

Office Gossip

HRCNM0905